RICHARD P. GLEASON

Sprout

First published by Bird with Fry Corp 2022

This novel is entirely a work of fiction. The names, characters and incidents portrayed in it are the work of the author's imagination. Any resemblance to actual persons, living or dead, events or localities is entirely coincidental.

Second edition

ISBN: 978-1-7371830-1-3

Advisor: Mette Gleason
Advisor: Brigitte Gleason
Advisor: Alyssa Sollenberger
Advisor: Colleen Norheim
Advisor: Stephanie Delibertis
Advisor: Robin Santangelo
Advisor: Karen Norheim
Advisor: Taylor Suzenski
Illustration by Taylor Suzenski

To:
Jack, who challenged me to believe;
Pep, who showed me how to believe;
And Mette, who gave me a reason to believe.
Thanks also to Mary M. and Robin S.

"Now is it known unto you that life is not as a vexation of spirit, nor that all under the sun is in vain; but rather that all things were and are ever marching toward truth."

—Kahlil Gibran

Contents

Foreword

The first time I read my uncle's book, *Sprout*, I was just a little girl of ten. I remember, then, thinking how wonderful the story was and how I would like to fill the story of my life with great adventures just like this story's hero, Woodsprout, does.

A few years ago around Christmas, I picked it up again. And I was struck, as an adult of forty-three, how much the story and life lessons still held true. I instantly wanted to share it with others but realized the book had long since been out of print.

In 2009, we lost my uncle to the throes of mental illness. Were he still alive, I am sure many more Sprout books would have come to life, and I could have asked him questions about how he developed this delightful story.

I had been toying with the idea of writing a book myself for some time but had not yet found my story. I started to think about my uncle and his book, *Sprout*, and all the wonderful life messages he wove into it. I thought how amazing it would be to republish *Sprout*, honoring my uncle and perhaps one day writing the next book in the Sprout series, expanding on Sprout's adventures and weaving in the lessons I have learned from my life.

My uncle left behind two beautiful and amazing daughters, my cousins Alyssa and Brigitte, as well as my good friend and aunt, Mette. I reached out and asked how they would feel if we published his book again together. This was the spark that lit our collective fire to share Richard's story and his book again with the world.

Together, we embarked on our own family adventure, soliciting advice and help from my mother, Colleen (Richard's sister); my sister, Stephanie (Richard's niece); and my uncle's close friend Rob. We also recruited my talented and artistic niece, Taylor, to work on illustrations.

This book is a celebration of a clever and witty-minded author, a loving and caring father, and a wise and inspiring uncle. I can imagine him sitting in his chair puffing on a pipe, thinking of us and our efforts, saying, "COOL BEANS! Well done, well done!"

Xxoo,
Karen Norheim, Richard's niece

Acknowledgement

We, the family and close friends of Richard Gleason, have rediscovered this book and find its messages just as important today as any day or time. We have pooled our skills, although none of us are writers, to republish an updated version that we hope will delight children as well as adults once again.

Mette Gleason, widow of Richard, critic, and supporter of the efforts
Alyssa Sollenberger, daughter of Richard, critic, and supporter of the efforts
Brigitte Gleason, daughter of Richard, critic, and supporter of the efforts
Robin Santangelo, close friend of Richard, critic, and supporter of the efforts
Colleen Norheim, sister of Richard, critic, and supporter of the efforts
Stephanie Norheim, niece, critic, and supporter of the efforts
Taylor Suzenski, niece-once-removed, Stephanie's daughter,
critic, and illustrator of this edition
Karen Norheim, niece, critic, and initiator of the project

This is a collaboration of all of us, our recollections, our thoughts and ideas, and our experiences with Richard, combined to bring forth this new edition.

"COOL BEANS!"

Chapter 1
A Most Wonderful Gift

Once upon a time, when time wasn't held to be so very important, a child was born, a child like most other children, born to parents like most other parents. In fact, except that this particular child is inseparable from this particular story, it could be safely said that the child was much the same as you and me.

The child's parents lived and worked on their own little farm. They were good people, and both were very pleased to be blessed with a child because they loved each other very much and had long prayed for one. So, too, they loved the child when he was born.

If the child had been a girl, the mother, who loved the deep, starry nights, would have named her "Gemstar" after her favorite star that hung high in the heavens like a blue-white diamond. But since the child was a boy, the father, who loved the rich brown soil and the green growing plants, chose to name their son "Woodsprout" and nicknamed him "Sprout" for short.

Since Sprout was like most children, loved and innocent, he did what infants do: he cried when he was hungry, smiled when he was happy, which was most of the time, and learned to crawl around and get into things he shouldn't. But *shouldn't* is a word, and infants do not know very much about words, so doing things they "shouldn't" isn't so very bad.

Sprout lived in a good home with good parents, and since a good home is like good growing soil for children, Sprout grew quickly, straight and true. He grew so fast, in fact, that his father was afraid that the roof would fall in on the house from all the notches he had to put in the center wooden beam to keep track of Sprout's height.

The years rolled by like fresh doughnuts down a growing boy's mouth. Sprout learned to play and laugh and help around the farm, when he wasn't eating doughnuts and other good things his mother always made. He learned words and their meanings and how to put them together to form sentences, some of which he liked very much: "Dinner's ready." "You can go out to play." "Good job!" Others he didn't like as much: "Don't do that!" "It's time for bed." "There is no more pie." But all in all, he liked very much being "Sprout" and he liked growing up.

After Sprout reached the age when he had to count his years by using more than the fingers on both hands, his father came to him carrying a gift wrapped in cloth.

"Sprout," his father began in a tone fathers use, "it's time that you start filling the pages of your life."

Sprout would have found the words very burdensome, indeed, if he hadn't been so awfully curious about what was wrapped in the cloth.

"Your mother and I gave you the best beginning we could, but now the rest of the story is going to be mostly up to you."

Having said this, Sprout's father pulled back the cloth and handed him a wondrous gift, an intricately handcrafted book bound in fine red leather. With eyes ablaze, Sprout eagerly accepted the book into his hands. To be sure, it was a most precious gift, for Sprout loved books. With all their magic and mystery, they opened like a private doorway to distant lands and faraway places with enchanted castles and brave, mighty deeds. Already Sprout was very fond of this beautiful book because it was to be the first that he could truly call his very own. How splendid to have a book all to oneself!

Eagerly but with great care, Sprout turned back the cover to the title page. There, to his still greater delight, in large lovely flowing script was written his name: Woodsprout. And just below that, his birth date. Quite beside himself with joy, Sprout turned to the next page, and the next, and the next, until his face was fixed in utter bewilderment. Except for the title page with his name and birth date, all the other pages were as blank and white as new fallen snow.

Confused, Sprout looked at his father. But his father only smiled and said, "As I told you, Sprout, your mother and I gave you the best beginning we could. Now it is up to you to fill the pages of your life, to write your own story."

Sprout could find no words to fill the gaping hollow left when his mouth dropped open. If the skin of his face had not held his jaw so well, Sprout's jaw might have fallen clear down to his ankles.

"You see, Sprout, each of us is born as a book of blank pages bound by life itself," his father explained. "Each of us must fill the pages of our own book with the life we live, for it is a tale to be written, a story to be told. This is the book of your life. It will be your story. So I hope you will write it carefully, because each page you write can never be erased or rewritten. That's the way of things."

After his father returned to his chores, Sprout gazed down upon his beautiful red book of blank pages and was more than a little perplexed.

Finally, after much wonderment, it occurred to Sprout that when confronted with a task, no matter how perplexing it seems at first, the best thing to do is to *do* something.

With that, Sprout went to his father, who was fast at work tilling the rich brown soil, thanked him again for the beautiful book, and told him he was going to begin the task of filling the pages of his life. Then Sprout found his mother in the kitchen and told her that he was going to make a beginning. She smiled warmly, in the way that only mothers can, then gave him a bright green cap in which was stuck a tall feathered quill. The cap and feather were her special gift—the cap to cover his head, and the feather, a clever combination of adornment and writing instrument.

So, with his new red book tucked safely in a little pack on his back, his small pocketknife in his pocket, and his green cap and feather on his head, Sprout set out into the world in search of stories to record in his life's book. And perhaps even an adventure or two. And, of course, Sprout knew he'd have to collect lots of words and sentences, because you can't write stories or adventures without them.

As he headed off down the lane toward the road leading to town, his mother called through the kitchen window. "Sprout, you be home before dinner. You hear?" Sprout turned back, waved to her, then started on his journey to begin the first chapter, hopefully an adventure, in the story of his life.

Chapter 2
A Matter of Adjectives

A s Sprout walked beneath the deep, clear blue sky, the rising morning sun spread its sparkling rays across the countryside like glistening sand cast into the wind. The road, which wound its way around hills, past fields, and over streams, was empty. But that didn't bother Sprout. Having traveled this way many times with his father, Sprout knew the road to town well enough. Yet, to be walking alone, with his new bright green cap with the tall feather and his little pack holding his beautiful red book of blank pages waiting to be filled, made the well-trodden way seem new and different.

It was not long before Sprout heard the *clap, clap* of a horse's hooves slapping the road behind him. Sprout turned to one side and watched the slow progress of the Miller's wagon piled high with sacks of milled grain.

The Miller sat hunched over behind the reins as if the full burden was upon his shoulders. His head hung so low, and was buried so deeply beneath a great floppy brown hat, that he would have surely driven right past Sprout with not so much as a nod of recognition if Sprout had not called out to him in a loud, friendly voice, "Good morning to you, Sir!"

Almost grudgingly, the Miller pulled up the reins and brought the wagon to a stop. From beneath the wide brim of his hat, the Miller's voice came like gravel kicked from a horse's angry hoof. "Good morning? *Good* morning? That may be easy enough for you to say, as you look to be out for a nice, pleasant morning's walk without a care in the world to trouble you. But I, you can plainly see, am hard at work, hauling this heavy load to town. It may be a good enough morning for you."

Still thrilled by the prospect of his life's story begun, Sprout was not offended by the sour tone in the Miller's voice. Sprout thought to point out to the Miller that it appeared as if it was, in fact, the horse that was doing most of the hauling. But Sprout did not because his father had told him that it is always best for young boys to treat elders with courteous respect. Instead, Sprout said to the Miller, "Begging your pardon, Sir, but I thought it a good morning because the weather is pleasant, and I have a fine new cap with a feather. It seemed to be a grand day to begin an important task that may take me a very long time to complete."

"And what important task could so young a fellow as you be about?" the Miller asked in the same gravelly voice.

Sprout pulled his beautiful book from his backpack and held it high so that the morning sun glistened across its bright red leather cover. "I have just begun the task of living, and I must fill the pages of my life book."

The Miller pushed his hat back upon his head, revealing a face that was not nearly as rough as his voice.

"And I was hoping," Sprout continued, "that if you have a moment or two to spare, you might consider lending me a few adjectives to put in my book. Gathering adjectives could be the proper way to begin, and I would imagine that any good story should have an ample supply of them." Sprout's eyes shone with the clear sparkle of a mountain spring beginning the long journey to the sea.

"So it's adjectives you're after," the Miller said, "and at a cost of a few moments of my time. That's a wagonload you ask. But I'm feeling generous this morning," the Miller said sarcastically. "So I'll tell you what I'm going to do. I won't lend you the adjectives; I'll *give* them to you. A young fellow like you ought to know what life's all about before he gets too far along with his writing. Maybe, then, you'll think twice before asking too much from life and from working people like me."

Sprout eagerly opened his book to the first page, then pulled the feathered quill from his hat and sat down upon the road's shoulder, ready to write. With a grim smile, the Miller recited a list of adjectives, which went like this:

weary
dreary
and all together bleary
woesome
loathsome
and particularly lonesome
sorrowful
mournful
and oh so tearful
belaboring
laboring
and always toiling

7

racked
worried
and decidedly brokenhearted
intolerable
insufferable
and positively unbearable
imperfect
inadequate
and most indifferent

The list went on for some time with no apparent end in sight. It was all Sprout could do to keep up since the Miller spoke ever faster in ever harsher tones like an avalanche set loose.

As Sprout recorded each adjective, its meaning began to show in his eyes, first clear and bright, then cloudy and sad, until tears threatened to spill down like overfilled glasses of water. Sprout had asked for adjectives and had gotten adjectives, but such adjectives that should not fill the first pages of the book of a young boy's life.

The Miller was not a bad man, nor had his life been more unduly hard than any other's. But, somehow, along the way, the Miller had begun to take note of more bad adjectives than good ones. And bad adjectives are tricky, sticky things, like candy. One or two aren't so harmful, used sparingly. But if you eat too much candy or use too many bad adjectives, your stomach soon begins to ache and you feel awful.

When the Miller stopped his list abruptly, Sprout looked up with his saltwatery eyes. Across the Miller's face came a warm and friendly smile, the first the Miller had shown in quite a long time. He said to Sprout, "You'll have to forgive this old miller for giving you all those nasty adjectives. It isn't at all a good way for you to begin your story. Now you come up on my wagon and ride to town with me, and I'll give you a list of proper good adjectives to work with."

Sprout looked up at the Miller with as much surprise as delight, and the boy's eyes sparkled again as they should.

"A story begun with good adjectives will have a better ending," the Miller said. "That's what my father once told me when I was just a lad starting out in life. Somehow I had forgotten that until now, and if I hadn't, then maybe I wouldn't be carrying around so many unpleasant ones."

The Miller reached down, lifted Sprout up, and set him down on the seat next to him. Remarkedly, the Miller was now sitting tall and straight as if he hauled no burden at all, and his face shone bright with the color of thriving fields of grain. He shook the reins, and the horse sprang forward into a walk as though the wagon were loaded with nothing more than caterpillar hairs. Sprout sat with his open book on his lap, quill in hand, waiting for the Miller to start a new list of adjectives.

"Let me see where to begin again," the Miller said. "How about with my wife? Now there is a woman who deserves as many good adjectives as a garden of daffodils."

bright
light
and what a delight
caring
bearing
and always pleasing
wholesome
growthsome
and needless to say suitably handsome
and who could ever doubt that she is
virtuous
courteous
and sincerely gracious
and fortunately, she is not belligerent,
even though
she is diligent
and easily intelligent

The list went on for several pages before they finally came to the Tavern at the edge of town. The Miller would often stop at the Tavern to drink a flagon of ale in an attempt to wash away the unpleasant taste left in his mouth from using all those bad adjectives. That, of course, never worked. But on this fine morning, the Miller wanted to celebrate the pleasing taste left from listing so many good adjectives for Sprout's book.

Chapter 3
Flagons and Dragons

W hen the Miller pulled his horse up in front of the Tavern, he asked Sprout, "Won't you come along inside with me and have a cold lemonade? And if you like stories, there's a famous knight who tells all who are willing to listen how he slew the terrible fire-breathing dragon." Smiling broadly, the Miller added, "In fact, what a story that is!"

It's well known everywhere that young boys love lemonade. But even better, they love tales of heroic knights slaying fire-breathing dragons. And Sprout was no exception. He leaped into the air with such excitement that it was a wonder his feet ever returned to the ground. To meet a knight who not only had seen a dragon but had actually done one in! What a great opportunity to use one of the Miller's adjectives and record a heroic story in his new book.

With Sprout anxiously prancing behind, the Miller led the way into the Tavern. As quickly as Sprout's eyes adjusted to the dim light, he scanned the morning crowd for a glimpse of the fearless knight in shining armor. The Miller made his way among the tables until he found an empty chair among a group of patrons with whom he often drank. Sprout followed along with eyes ever searching.

Finally, after the Miller had ordered a mug of ale and a pint of lemonade, Sprout could not contain himself any longer. He tugged upon the Miller's arm. "Excuse me, Sir, but where is the dragon-slaying knight? I surely don't want to miss seeing a real hero."

The others at the table, hearing Sprout's request, broke out in a chorus of loud laughter and pointed over to the one empty corner in the Tavern.

Sprout wound his way across until he came to an area that was deserted except for a sleeping figure sprawled in a chair. The figure was dressed in armor sure enough, but it was a suit of armor so rusty and tarnished that it looked as if the man inside had been swallowed whole up to his head by an old potbellied stove badly soiled from use. Or in the case of armor, nonuse. The Knight's head, cocked to one side, was nearly hidden by two flabby cheeks and a great knobby nose out of which came long, loud snores that were the rival of any herd of fat bullfrogs roaring on a summer's eve.

At first, Sprout thought some mistake had been made, that this could not possibly be a dragon-slaying knight. But above and behind the Knight's head, on a wooden plaque fastened to the wall, carved in large bold letters was the title Dragon Slayer. Beneath that, someone had scrawled on the wall with a piece of charcoal, "And slayer of many a flagon."

So inexplicable did it all seem that Sprout dared to step closer to the Knight. Tapping on the front of the armor as if tapping on an apple barrel to see

13

if someone is hiding within, Sprout asked, "Excuse me, Sir. Are you the dragon-slaying knight?"

Suddenly, in midsnore, the eyes opened, the head jerked upright, and a voice that sounded more frightened than brave bellowed, "Dragon? Dragon! Where?"

The Knight might have risen to his feet either to make ready for a dragon's onslaught or to flee, but the armor was so rusted that the Knight managed only to make a great clatter of squeaks and rusty groans without leaving the chair at all. His eyes blinked wildly until they focused upon little Sprout with his backpack, green cap, and tall feathered quill.

The noise the rusty armor had made was so awful that Sprout had jumped back a step and held his ears until the clatter, like the crash of an avalanche of pots and pans falling to the floor, subsided.

Mistaking Sprout's actions for fear, the Knight gurgled a laugh and said, "That's right, lad. You should jump back from a terrible knight when you're foolish enough to wake him unexpectedly. I could have accidentally done away with you as quick as a fly beats its wings."

In afterthought, the Knight attempted to reach across to the sword at his waist, but the rusted joints of his armor prevented him from so abrupt an action. Instead, he resorted to banging his other arm, which moved easily enough, upon the table next to him. This sent a score or more of the empty flagons that covered the tabletop crashing to the floor. "lnnkeep! lnnkeep!" the Knight bellowed. "A flagon of ale for the Dragon Slayer."

The lnnkeep soon appeared, more annoyed than pleased, and set down a large flagon of ale for the Knight. The Knight had been granted unlimited access to the Tavern's finest ale as one of the privileges the townspeople had bestowed upon the Dragon Slayer for ridding the town and countryside of a terrible nuisance. And if you've ever met a real-live fire-breathing dragon face-to-face, or even just had one running loose in your backyard, you surely know what a terrible nuisance such a creature can be.

As Sprout looked on, the Knight raised the flagon to his mouth, unleashing a wide spray of suds amid long, loud gulps. The Knight's aim was so dreadful that he managed to pour as much ale down into his suit of armor as into his mouth. This resulted in a number of little sprays of ale, leaking from the armor's joints like an old rusty bucket of water with holes. Sprout thought this ridiculously funny, but he did not laugh out loud for, after all, a knight is a knight, and that should account for something.

When the Knight had drained the ale down to the last slurp, he banged the flagon on the table, sending another set of empty flagons crashing to the floor. The Knight's behavior struck Sprout as a rather poor display, especially for someone reported to be so heroic.

"Now then, lad. A tale of dragon-slaying I'm going to tell you," the Knight boomed. "A tale as great and mighty as any ever told."

The Knight proceeded, employing painstaking care to pinpoint the most minute details concerning himself, regardless of how little it mattered to the story.

Excluding the extra wording, like so much wrapping on a Christmas present, the tale went like this:

The evil fire-breathing Dragon lived in a very nasty cave at the foot of a mountain, not far from the town and its surrounding countryside. He traveled all over this countryside, because, if you didn't know, dragons travel very fast, indeed.

For a long while, the Dragon wasn't much of an annoyance to the townspeople, because, you see, dragons don't like to live in houses. Even with their wings folded, they can't get much more than their fearsome big heads through a doorway. And, too, dragons hate the sound of singing and dancing, which townsfolk like to do quite often, because dragons with their big, clawed feet and fat bellies can't dance, and with their voices that boom like thunder, they can't even stand to listen to themselves sing.

Once in a while, the Dragon did anger the farmers because when he was feeling naughty, the Dragon, roaring loudly, liked to swoop down very low over the heads of grazing sheep and cattle. Needless to say this frightened the herds badly and sent them bounding in all directions, which, in turn, took the farmers all day to calm and gather. And when the Dragon had a particularly irritating itch on his fat belly beneath his steel-like scales, which even his sharp claws couldn't scratch, he would get to feeling exceptionally nasty and go rampaging through an apple orchard, scorching trees, or stomping through neat rows of corn.

The Dragon did that kind of thing just to make the farmers angry and to have others share in his own misery of having an itch that couldn't be scratched. But despite those sorts of irritating pranks, no farmer ever got quite angry enough to go tell the Dragon about it. Which was probably a smart thing, for dragons don't like to be scolded for their bad behavior. Considering the possibilities, a few scorched apple trees or a few stomped rows of corn weren't so hard to learn to put up with. As to the children, after the Dragon had done his mischief, it was a great treat to eat freshly toasted apples and quick-roasted corn, which is probably how popcorn was discovered.

All in all, the townspeople and the farmers got along well enough with the Dragon. That is, as well as anyone could be expected to get along with a fire-breathing dragon lurking nearby. But one day, as the townspeople were celebrating Midsummer's Eve with much singing and dancing, as was their custom, the Dragon did something that was entirely unacceptable.

On that day, the Dragon had an enormously annoying itch beneath his scales and nothing seemed to satisfy his irritation. Not even scorching an entire orchard of apple trees was enough. Flying near the town looking for some mischief to perform, the Dragon heard the joyous singing and music of the Midsummer's celebration. With his unscratchable itch causing him so much misery and the people singing and dancing and having so much fun, the Dragon positively could not stand to have others happy when he was not.

And so, with a great flapping of wings, the Dragon swooped down upon the townspeople who were merrymaking at the center of town and snatched from their midst the Fair Maid of Honor chosen for the holiday. With another beating of his great wings like a hurricane loosed, the Dragon leaped back into the sky with the Maiden in his clutches.

After the Dragon was well out of sight, the townspeople raised themselves from the ground where they had been sprawled in fear. Looking up to make sure the Dragon was nowhere to be seen, the townspeople erupted into a long refrain of indignations.

Something must be done. But what? No one was eager to volunteer to do anything until someone pointed to the Knight. A chorus of cheers arose. A Knight! A Knight! Dealing with wayward dragons was a task fit for a knight. All agreed on that. The Mayor took it upon himself to approach the Knight and bestow upon him the duty of evicting the Dragon from the neighborhood and returning the Maiden. For performing that small favor, the Mayor assured the Knight that the whole town would be duly grateful and ample reward would be granted. With that, the townspeople bid the Knight farewell and quickly returned to their homes and farms, taking care to lock the doors and windows behind them.

Left alone in the town square, the Knight had no one to see him on his way. But what matter was that? A task was at hand for a brave and fearless Knight to evict a bad-mannered dragon and rescue a fair maiden.

Meanwhile the Dragon flew to his nasty cave beneath the mountain and carefully set the Maiden down unhurt before the entrance. The Maiden, of course, was frightened and lay very still.

Why dragons steal fair maidens, or what they intend to do with them, no one can say. It's just something typical of dragons when they're being bad. Slouched as he was in a heap at the cave's entrance, amid deep brooding puffs of smoky vapor, the Dragon himself was probably trying to figure out what to do with the Maiden now that he had her. And that is precisely how the Knight found them when he finally came to the foot of the mountain.

Sprout watched as the Knight paused in the telling of his dragon-slaying adventure to drain another flagon of ale. Then, as the Knight told it, the tale went on something like this: the Knight, being brave and fearless and knowing his duty to the townspeople and his code of honor, raised his gleaming sword on high, shouted a holy oath, and charged the Dragon.

No one had ever dared to approach the Dragon on his doorstep and that, in itself, took the Dragon by surprise. But facing a fearless knight in shining armor with a bright sword raised menacingly to strike was too much for the Dragon. He turned, and leaving the Maiden behind, fled into his dark, nasty cave. The Knight, resolute in his promise to evict the Dragon, followed him in. A chase ensued in which the Dragon fled down the long twisting labyrinth of his cave with the mighty Knight following close behind.

When the Dragon finally reached the very heart and root of the mountain and could flee no farther, he turned to confront the pursuing Knight. What followed was a battle of fire and steel to rival any battle Knight and Dragon had ever fought. As the Dragon inhaled deeply, the Knight swept with his sword, pushing the Dragon back. He then quickly jumped behind a large rock, just moments before the Dragon exhaled his next fiery breath. Feeling the heat of the rock, the Knight contemplated if his next breath would be his last. Bravely, he shuffled to the edge of the rock to see the Dragon and plan his attack. Luck was on his side that day, as the Dragon was distracted by his unscratchable itch. Without hesitation, the Knight saw his chance and sprang upon the Dragon.

In the end, at the dark center of the mountain, the Knight was victorious and the Dragon was slain.

Making his way back up through the cave, the Knight then returned the Maiden to the townspeople. A tremendous celebration followed in which the Knight received his just rewards. Or so the Knight said.

By the time the Knight had gotten to the end of his tale, his last sentences were delivered with his head nodding forward. Soon the Knight was deep in a sleep of the kind that comes from a tale too long and too often told.

For a while young Sprout looked on at the Knight in his rusty armor and his large protruding nose from which issued the most awful snores. Throughout the telling, Sprout had found it difficult to relate the Knight he saw before him with the Knight in the tale.

Shortly the Miller came up to Sprout, and laying a gentle hand upon Sprout's shoulder asked, "Well, lad, have you heard a good story?"

Turning to the Miller, Sprout said, "I'm not quite sure what I have heard, if you understand what I mean. A good story it was, but seeing the Knight, something doesn't seem quite right."

The Miller laughed good-naturedly. "You're a bright boy, and you deserve to know the difference between a good story and a *good* story. I've heard the Knight tell his version more than I care to, and up to the point where the Dragon steals the Maiden away, his story is true enough. But from there on, another version of the tale needs telling."

The Miller went on to say that after the Dragon had flown away with the Maiden, the townspeople found the Knight, who had been celebrating very heavily among the ale barrels, cowering beneath a table with a flagon in each hand. The townspeople were so insistent that he do something about the Dragon that the Knight knew he had little choice in the matter. In turn, the Mayor had been so upset by the whole incident that when he instructed the Knight which direction the Dragon's cave lay, he told the Knight to go west, when in fact the Dragon's mountain was in the east.

After the Mayor and other folk had sped back to their homes, curiously enough the Knight headed east. What a surprise the Knight must have had when the road he thought he was on turned out to come, after a sharp bend, right at the foot of the Dragon's mountain, with the Dragon parked on the doorstep.

The Dragon, as you know, was not in a good mood that day, and when a knight showed up at his front door, he became altogether dragonly. That is, he became most unruly and of an irate temperament to do something very unpleasant to anyone who crossed his path, much less appear at his cave quite uninvited and most unwanted.

Suddenly the Dragon leaped into the air with a mind to give the Knight a good scorching, sword or no sword. And to a full-grown dragon with his steely scales and sharp claws, a sword in the hands of a knight, especially that Knight, is little more than a rib tickler or a back scratcher.

As the Dragon took to the air with a light in his eye that was altogether fearsome, the Knight fully realized the situation he had inadvertently wound up in. With little desire to tangle with a dragon, much less try to evict an angry one, the Knight turned and began to run. But running in armor is not so easy to do. Just as the Dragon was in the midst of a full-speed swoop down upon the Knight, the Knight tripped over his dangling sword and fell flat upon his face. Issuing a full blast of his fiery breath, the Dragon overshot the prostrate Knight. The Dragon had been so angry and had been flying so fast that, upon missing the Knight, the Dragon crashed right into a lake that lay near the foot of the mountain.

As you can guess, dragon's aren't particularly clean animals and as a result don't like water very much. And as you surely must know, fire and water don't mix. So when the Dragon hit the lake with his mouth wide open, water poured in and drowned out the fire inside him. Once a dragon's fire is extinguished, which takes a great deal of water, he can never start it again. And a dragon without his fire is nothing more than a big lizard.

A great cloud of mist and fog hung over the lake as the Dragon managed to struggle back to the shore. Without his fire to scare people and toast apple trees and popcorn, the Dragon was a timid and cowardly creature. He could not stand to face anyone who wouldn't be afraid of him. And so, dripping wet and with tail curled up behind him, the Dragon slunk back into his cave and descended to the mountain's depths and was never seen again.

"But how do you know that the Knight's story was not true since the Maiden was in a faint?" Sprout asked with a dejected look on his face.

"I saw the Knight as he returned to town. His face mask and the front of his armor were scratched and pitted with gravel from his fall, while the back of his armor was blackened where the Dragon's fire had touched as he flew over. And a farmer who lived not far from the other side of the lake had seen the great cloud of vapor rise when the Dragon crashed into the lake."

"Didn't the townspeople realize that?" Sprout asked.

"Perhaps some did, but most were just happy to have the Dragon quieted and the Maiden returned. They let the Knight tell his tale, and, for a while, anyway, they treated him as if he had done what he said he had, and as if he were a hero."

"But why?" Sprout asked.

"Because people like to believe in heroes even if they don't really have one, and they like to believe in a good story, even if it isn't true. After a while, though, most people pieced together the truth, and so the Knight became what you see," the Miller said, pointing to the snoring pile of metal and flesh.

Sprout looked down at his own feet, feeling sorely disappointed. He, too, would have liked to believe the tale as the Knight had told it. But he could not, and that made him very sad.

"You see, lad, a good story can be about good people doing good things that actually happened, and a good story can be about good things and people that isn't true and didn't happen. Even people like the Knight, who aren't so good, can tell a good story, true or not. A good story is always a good story whether or not it actually happened. You have to take it for what it is."

"But shouldn't people who tell good stories let you know if it's a true good story or just a good story?" Sprout asked.

"You're learning, lad," the Miller said with a smile. "That's the whole point. Be truthful about whatever you say. The difference between a person who tells the truth about what he is saying and someone who doesn't is the same as the difference between a Dragon Slayer and a Flagon Slayer," the Miller said, pointing to the sign above the sleeping Knight in rusty armor.

Sprout said goodbye to the Miller and thanked him for the contributions to his book, especially for all the good adjectives. Once outside the Tavern and by himself, Sprout carefully entered the entire episode into his lovely red book. He was still sadly disappointed, though, because he had wanted very much to have a hero in his book. When a young boy seeks a hero and finds only a Flagon Slayer, it is a very disappointing thing indeed.

Putting his feathered quill back into his green cap and his red book back into his pack, Sprout headed on into town to a place where he knew he could find things to add to his book that he knew would be true. And what could be truer than facts and knowledge? And what better place to find facts and knowledge than in a library?

Chapter 4
Knowledge and Dancing Elephants

The Library stood near the town square, but unlike the town square, people seemed to walk around it, almost avoiding it, even though entry was free to all. This Sprout never understood. His father had told him that knowledge was like rich soil to corn and spring rain to grass, that it made the mind grow. It was strange that something free and so good for people as knowledge was so often passed up for the pursuit of other things costly and hard to acquire, like gold and jewelry. It was a question that was on Sprout's mind as he climbed the steps and entered through the great oaken doors of the Library.

When Sprout crossed the threshold, he nearly fell over the outstretched legs of a figure fast asleep on a stool by the door. Taken by surprise, the sleeping figure jumped immediately to his feet and Sprout found himself staring up into the eyes of a boy perhaps not much older than himself but at least half a head taller.

"Who are you?" Sprout asked in a tone that sounded like a challenge, though he hadn't intended so.

"Why, I am the Door-Keep of the Library, the Great Hall of Knowledge," the boy said, proudly thrusting his chest forward. "And who are you?" the Door-Keep asked. "And what do you want here?"

The Door-Keep was exceptionally lanky for his age, and of a build that suggests a body askew with the mind that moves it, as if calamity is only a movement away.

"My name is Sprout, and I'm here to find knowledge," Sprout said, in a more friendly tone.

"So that's what you're after, is it?" the Door-Keep asked with a suspicious smile. "You've come to the right place. But you'll have to speak with the Librarian first. She's in charge of all knowledge here."

Sprout turned to gaze upon the vast vaulted interior of the Library, with its level upon level of shelves brimming with books soaring up into the dim, unfathomable heights above. Sprout was truly awed by what he saw. He could never have imagined that there could be so many books in the entire world, much less so many in one place.

Appreciating the amazement spread across Sprout's face, the Door-Keep smiled broadly with immense pride. "Someday, I'll be the Chief Librarian and be in charge of this great domain of knowledge."

"Wow," Sprout said with admiration and a little envy. "Are you allowed to read anything you want?" he asked.

The Door-Keep pointed to a stack of books by the stool where he had been dozing. "Not only allowed to—I have to read. That's how you become a librarian, by reading and learning to find your way around books, where they go, how they are organized, and a great deal more than that."

A bond of affection had already sprung up between Sprout and the Door-Keep. "Come along," the Door-Keep said to Sprout. "We'd best find the Librarian."

With that, the Door-Keep set off across the library floor in steps so jerky that Sprout was afraid that with the next step the Door-Keep's lanky legs might set off in separate directions, leaving the rest of the body to get about without their aid. He led Sprout past rows upon rows of book-filled shelves, up creaky stairs, along book-lined passages, till Sprout thought that without the Door-Keep to lead, he might become lost in this complex maze for a thousand years.

Finally, they came upon a tiny little woman in a dim book-packed nook mumbling to herself as she arranged various volumes upon the shelf. "No, no, that will never do, you tricky dear. You're always appearing where you shouldn't be," she said, plucking a book from the shelf. Stroking it fondly, she made a place for it between two others. "Prestidigitation belongs before prevarication, now no fibbing you, and after presbyopia, you poor dear; you can never see who you're near."

On the top of the Librarian's head was a bun so messy and disheveled that it reminded Sprout of a bird's nest.

"Ma'am, " the Door-Keep began, "there is someone here in search of knowledge, and I thought it best that—"

The old Librarian whirled suddenly, and without letting the Door-Keep finish, exclaimed, "Hey! Knowledge! Knowledge, you say? Knowledge, indeed. That is true enough. Why, knowledge is what libraries are all about, or, rather," she made a sweeping gesture to the endless array of books, "I should say knowledge is all about a library." As if only just recognizing Sprout's guide, the Librarian commanded, "Door-Keep, what are you doing here? Haven't you learned yet that a door-keep's job, which is what you are supposed to be doing, is to be at the door? Now get along with you."

The young lad turned and, with a wink to Sprout, disappeared into the maze of bookshelves. Feeling as if he were before someone very important and knowledgeable, Sprout took off his cap in a sign of respect.

Taking a step forward, the Librarian began to study Sprout with eyes that loomed huge behind a pair of thick spectacles set most precariously on the very edge of her nose. "Knowledge, you're after? Well, well. You're a young one to be after so immense a thing as knowledge, but no one's too young to begin that search. No, indeed. As a matter of fact, the sooner one gets started, the closer one gets to never having it." The Librarian concluded with a dusty laugh.

"Ma'am?" Sprout said, not understanding what the Librarian meant by her last statement.

"The more knowledge you have the more you know you don't have," the Librarian stated. "You see all these books? Now, if you read all of them, every one, and understand all that is in them, then and only then would you know that you really hadn't learned anything at all. Or not much, anyway."

"Ma'am?" Sprout repeated.

"Gad, son. Haven't you been listening? You're like that Door-Keep of mine, always wanting to know but never bothering to learn." The Librarian carefully took a huge book from a shelf. "Excuse me, dear, for disturbing your nice bed," she said lovingly to the book. "This is a book on 'primulaceous.' That's the family of flowers called 'primrose.' Now, if you read this book, you'd know a great deal more about a primrose than before, but far less than any bumblebee could tell you if he'd take time from his busy buzzing to bother to tell you anything at all. And if all the books in this library were all about primulaceous and each different, you wouldn't know half of what a primrose knows about itself, and that's a great deal if you've ever heard them gabbing away as they bob their heads in a breeze. The realm of knowledge is so immense that all the books in all the libraries in all the world wouldn't amount to more than the tiniest tip of the first letter in the first word in *The Book of All Knowledge.*"

Sprout suddenly felt very small and very insignificant, and it showed.

"Now, now, son. Don't start shrinking away," the Librarian said, reassuringly. "There is no reason not to start on the search for knowledge. It's just that you ought to know how long the road is."

Sprout felt a little better. "Do you mean, Ma'am, that seeking knowledge is like chasing after a sunset?"

The old Librarian's eyes blinked larger than ever. "Why, yes! That's good. You've taken your first step. Like the sunset, you'll never catch knowledge,

28

but that shouldn't stop you from learning and enjoying along the way." She turned and replaced the book. "Back you go, my dear, into your bed until you're plucked again. We've talked a little about knowledge, sure enough, but do you know what knowledge is?" the Librarian asked, turning her attention again to Sprout.

"Not exactly," Sprout admitted.

"When you're after something, it's best to know exactly what it is you're after. And the best place to begin most things begun well is at the beginning. Which is where most things begun begin."

At that Sprout took his book from his pack and his feathered quill from his green cap and sat down on a nearby stool.

"Knowledge begins with the naming of things. We call a tree a tree, a horse a horse. We've all come to agree upon the same name for the same things, and that is a marvelous accomplishment in itself. And mighty convenient, too, for if I were building a house and I said to you 'hammer,' and you thought by the word *hammer* I meant 'tomato,' I might be left trying to pound a nail with a tomato and that would prove messy in the least."

Sprout tried to refrain from laughing in front of so knowledgeable a person as the Librarian, but he could not help but giggle at the thought of trying to pound a nail with a tomato.

Behind her thick glasses, the Librarian's eyes blinked like shades on a window. She had not thought that anything she said was funny. She continued anyway.

"So you see, agreeing on the names of things is essential, and the names of things are nouns. *The* tree, *the* book, *the* cow, for specific things. Trees, books, cows, for groups of things, and *a* tree, *a* book, *a* cow for any single member of a general group. If we think of knowledge as a house for our thoughts and minds to live in, nouns are bricks. But a pile of bricks by itself is not a house nor is it a good place to call home. And a pile of nouns is no more knowledge than a pile of bricks.

"So to build knowledge, we have to begin by gathering an ample stock of nouns and then learn to put them together properly. If you take nouns and fasten them with a verb and adjective, you can fashion for yourself a complete statement." The Librarian waved a short, skinny finger at Sprout. "Now, mind you, you can't just put together two bricks any old way. You have to do it in a way that fits; otherwise, the house will crumble before you get the foundation started. To fit into the house of knowledge, the statement must be true, or, as knowledgeable people say of proper statements, valid."

"Could you give me an example of a true statement, Ma'am?" Sprout asked.

"I'm coming to that. Be patient."

The Librarian picked up Sprout's green cap and held it aloft as if it were now something very important. Pointing to it, the Librarian declared, as though evoking some powerful incantation, "The green hat is not blue."

To folks like you and me who have enough common sense to be able to tell an apple from an orange or a fairy from a troll, the Librarian's statement made about as much sense as saying that a herd of elephants cannot possibly tap dance on the head of a pin. For young Sprout, the Librarian's statement was so obviously true that he jumped like an elephant onto a pin without the slightest bit of patience or practice.

"But that's silly!" Sprout cried. "Anybody can see that!"

The Librarian's eyes spread wide like twin moons over the horizon as Sprout, remembering his manners, added, "Begging your pardon, Ma'am."

"Silly? Silly, you say!" the Librarian exclaimed. "Young people ought to learn about what they think they know before they speak, or better yet, just think before they speak. Of course, what I said is true, and it's obvious to all; green hats are never blue. That's the whole point. Even if you should argue long and hard for days on end, it does not change the fact that your green hat is not blue. Knowledge begins with true statements, and true statements are true no matter how you look at them.

"Now, not all statements are that obvious. Some take years of study to learn and understand. Like, did you know that the sum of the angles of a triangle is always equal to 180 degrees?"

"No," answered Sprout sheepishly, a little ashamed for his elephant jump.

"Well, it's true and as valid a statement as that your green hat is green. Valid statements are true because, regardless of who questions them, with enough study and clear thinking, they always turn out true. A true statement is a little bit of knowledge, a well-placed arrangement of bricks for the building of the house of knowledge."

The Librarian pointed her finger at Sprout and asked, "If I say that all verbs are words, and that all complete sentences have verbs in them, would you then agree that, therefore, all sentences contain words?"

Sprout thought for a long moment, trying to find an exception to the Librarian's statement. But, of course, he couldn't. "Why, yes, I have to agree, Ma'am, because it is true; all sentences *do* have words."

The Librarian smiled. "You thought before you spoke, and that's a very good habit. Statements can be valid, even if they aren't to be found in the physical world. If I say that only dwarfs can grow green beards, and that all dwarfs have beards, you can be sure that behind every green beard you will find a dwarf."

"Because one statement depends upon the other?" Sprout said with the growing excitement that comes with understanding.

"Why, yes, dear boy! You are beginning to think clearly, and don't you see that knowledge comes of clear thinking?" the Librarian asked cheerfully.

"In the house of knowledge," the Librarian continued, "as a roof is dependent upon sturdy walls, knowledge is dependent upon and built up by true statements, all held together by clear thinking. Clear thinking and diligent study are keys that will allow you to enter the house of knowledge so that you may explore its many rooms, marvel at the furnishings, and even discover new rooms. In fact, the house of all knowledge is so large that you could spend endless lives in just trying to learn what knowledge is already known, and an endless succession of endless lives in discovering what can be learned. And then, you'd have only just begun to explore the first floor."

"And you, Ma'am," Sprout added, referring to the huge, vaulted chamber of the book-filled library, "are the caretaker of a single room in that great house of all knowledge."

"You are becoming a dear, a little book in yourself, and someday when you finish filling your nice red book, you may find that it, too, should deserve a place among all the other dear books in this wonderful place."

Sprout beamed with unspoken pride. To think that his little red book could possibly someday deserve to sit with the other books was an awesome thing.

But just then a very disturbing thought occurred to Sprout. Even if the little book he was writing did some day deserve to sit among the other volumes in the library, who would read it? Only the Librarian and the Door-Keep? No one else ever appeared to come to the library even though it was open and free to all.

"Ma'am," Sprout asked the Librarian, "what good are all these books and all this knowledge if no one comes to learn and no one ever puts the knowledge to good use?"

Like an unsuspecting bear cub who sticks his unwary nose into a bee's hive, Sprout loosed a swarm of angry buzzing sentences from the Librarian. "What good is knowledge? Why, knowledge is its own best use, its own master, its own end. Used or not, knowledge is the foundation upon which the whole universe is built and upon which it runs!"

Before Sprout's fear-filled eyes, the Librarian began to dance about wildly, frantically waving her arms as if, in fact, she were beset by a swarm of disturbed bees. And Sprout had good reason to be afraid. Beneath the messy nest of the Librarian's towering bun lay a vast depository of knowledge. Knowledge is a very powerful force, and Sprout could scarcely imagine what terrible things the power of knowledge could do when used in anger or malice. Yet, as knowledgeable as the Librarian was, she did not have a bad bone in her; she was as good a soul as they come.

After a considerably long spell of ranting, the Librarian began to slow like an old clock when its gears bog down with the thickening stuff of time. Striking a last chime to the importance of knowledge, the Librarian came to an abrupt halt.

Following an appropriate span of silence, Sprout ventured to say, ever so respectfully, "Excuse my lack of knowing, Ma'am, but what I had meant to say would have been better put by asking why so few people ever come to take advantage of the great wealth of knowledge that is accumulated here."

The Librarian's large eyes blinked closed behind her thick glasses. "Ah, my dear, that is a question of a question, a question whose answer is a question. It appears that most people don't seek answers here at the Library because they don't ask questions. And that is a pity; for most have not yet realized that the true answer to living is a question."

Sprout tilted his head to one side as if to make sure that all of what the Librarian said sank in.

"You see, my dear," the Librarian continued, "living *is* questioning. We must question to live. All of us question and answer our way along through life until, in the end, all our questions are answers and all our answers are the greatest question of all: *Why?*"

Now, all this about questions and answers had gotten so out of hand that Sprout couldn't tell heads from tails, or dandelions from porcupines. But gaining knowledge from knowledgeable people isn't always as easy as picking dandelions. It's more often like trying to figure out which end of a porcupine to pick up without getting stuck. And that isn't exactly an easy thing to do.

But before Sprout had time to ask the Librarian to help sort matters out, the bell atop the town hall nearby was clanging out its noon message.

"Oh, my dear," the Librarian exclaimed, throwing up her hands. "It is twelve o'clock and time for the Library to close until later. That's enough for today. You'll have to run along now."

The Librarian shooed Sprout on his way with such haste that Sprout was barely able to gather his hat and quill and book and pack fast enough. Being quite honest, which is always best, Sprout was relieved to be scurrying along by himself among the piles and rows of books. Enough knowledge is enough at one sitting, and Sprout had swallowed about as much as his poor spinning head could handle.

But without the Librarian to show the way, Sprout was soon hopelessly lost in the maze of shelves and aisles. He actually became fearful that the great oaken front doors would be closed and locked, and that he would be shut in until all the answers became questions. And that, in the least, might take a very, very long time.

When he was just about to give up hope of ever finding his way out, Sprout rounded a corner and found himself facing the gangly shape of the Door-Keep.

"So there you are!" the Door-Keep said, with a friendly smile. "Got lost in all this knowledge, did you?" Without waiting for Sprout's reply, the Door-Keep led off with his lanky legs flying out this way and that, in a stride that proved difficult for Sprout to keep up with.

Trotting along behind, Sprout said, "Thank you for finding me and showing me the way. I was afraid I'd be shut in and never get out."

Over his shoulder, the Door-Keep said, "Knowledge can do that to a person, keep them shut in. Knowledge needs lots of sunshine to keep it clear and healthy."

Sprout thought about this for a moment, not really sure what to make of it until the Door-Keep added, "Knowledge is good enough in itself, but it's even better when it's taken out into the world and put to good use."

The Door-Keep's words made such plain, simple sense that Sprout let loose a loud fun-filled stream of laughter, which, when joined by the Door-Keep's, spread out and filled the great vaulted hall, making its dim heaviness a little lighter and a lot brighter.

With a final turn, the Door-Keep brought Sprout to the front entrance. They bade each other a warm goodbye, and Sprout promised that he would return when he could, and together they would explore the Library and marvel at the limitless wonders of knowledge.

Chapter 5
A Very Long Shortcut

As the huge oaken doors of the Library banged closed behind him, Sprout stepped out into the warm sunshine. He was feeling very good about himself for having added several more pages to his book. He had collected quite a list of adjectives and a tale of a hero (even though not from a real hero, which was a little disappointing), and he had learned a great deal about nouns, statements, and something of knowledge.

As with all boys, especially those hard at the task of filling the pages of the book of their lives, Sprout's stomach began a mumbling grumble that came from not eating since breakfast. And here it was, all the way to lunchtime.

Sprout decided it was time to head back home where a grumbling stomach can always find peace with fresh bread and pieces of cold sliced beef, and maybe a leftover slice of pie or two.

Trotting along, Sprout was soon at the edge of town where the road winds out across the countryside. For a while, the road ran next to the Old Forest and around its edge until home wasn't more than a couple of fields and a hill or so away. Passing beneath the outermost eaves of the forest's tall ancient trees, Sprout paused at a path that dove in among the towering pillars and the thick green roof above.

Sprout took cognizance of his growling stomach and concluded that this might be a shortcut to lunch.

Soon Sprout's feet were crunching down upon the dried leaves that covered the forest path. The trees appeared to grow taller and thicker the deeper he penetrated the forest. After what seemed a very long time, Sprout slowed his pace and his thoughts began to regain control over his moaning stomach. By his reckoning, Sprout was sure that by now he ought to have reached the other side and be looking out on the wide fields near his home. But as he peered into the thick array of towering trees, he could see no end to the Old Forest.

Once a little sense had come into his thinking, Sprout began to wonder if he hadn't made a mistake in being so hasty. And as we all know, haste doesn't always take you where you think it will. And that was just what Sprout was coming to realize when he came to a Y in the paths, each way looking about the same as the other.

In case you didn't know, a choice between two unknown paths is just the sort of thing that begins adventures. Choices that you never thought you'd have to make pop up in front of you, and before you ever even realize that you're in an adventure, one begins.

As Sprout was trying to decide whether to take the left path or the right, or to retrace the long way back, he spied what looked like the corner of a sign half hidden by an overhang of unruly ivy. Pushing aside the thick green leaves, Sprout discovered a sign that read: "Shortcut to where you'll find yourself when you get there," with an arrow beneath pointing to the left path. The sign didn't make all that much sense, but a shortcut is a shortcut, and that is exactly what Sprout had been looking for in the first place. So with renewed speed, Sprout headed along the path to the left.

Sprout had not gone very far when he heard what sounded like weeping coming from somewhere farther ahead. Where you find weeping you'll often find someone in need, and Sprout knew that helping someone in need was a good thing to do. Off Sprout went. Rounding a bend, Sprout came suddenly upon a young girl crying into her hands. Her blaze of long golden hair shone brightly in a shaft of sunlight that broke through the dense roof of the forest above. The girl did not take notice of Sprout's arrival until he bent down and touched her gently upon the shoulder. She dropped her hands and lifted her face, revealing deep blue eyes misted over by a veil of sparkling tears. Sprout was so taken that he immediately asked, "Is there anything, anything at all, that I can do to help?"

"I fear only a brave knight or a good wizard could help," the girl replied, with deep sadness and a heavy sigh.

"I am neither; but I would still like to help, if I can," Sprout offered.

The golden-haired girl studied Sprout for a moment, then seeing his honest intentions, told him her plight. The young girl lived alone with her mother in a little cottage far from town and the nearest neighbor, but not far from the edge of the Old Forest. One day, the girl's mother took ill and was forced to stay in bed while the young girl did the daily chores and did her best to look after her mother. As the days passed, her mother grew worse until she fell into a deep, fitful fever.

The girl became very worried, for there was nothing she could do, and it was so very far to town. When her mother began to take a turn for the worse, the girl knew she must get help. Nearly desperate, the young girl took the meager sum of their savings, and leaving her mother with bread and soup by the bed in case she should awake, she set out to find the wise and good wizard that was rumored to live in the Old Forest. The Wizard, it was told, possessed power and means to cure.

Soon after entering the forest, the girl became hopelessly lost among the dense trees and unmarked trails. As she walked aimlessly, growing more fearful all the time for her sick mother, the girl passed a tree stump that spoke out to her. In actuality it was not a tree stump at all but rather a short, squat fellow all dressed in brown and answering to the name Toad, which, from his odd appearance and strange half hop, half walking gait, fit him well enough for a name.

Toad, guessing that she was lost, asked the girl her business. She told him that she was looking for the Good Wizard to ask of him a cure for her sick mother. And, too, she told Toad that she had four gold coins to appropriately pay the Wizard for services rendered.

It was an innocent enough thing to say, but it turned out to be the very worst thing to disclose to this particular fellow. Toad told the girl that the supposed Good Wizard was actually a bad sort who couldn't even help himself to dinner, much less help anyone who was really sick. Instead, he said that there was a kindly old woman who lived nearby, who was skilled in herb lore and could surely help. And, he added, that for a single gold coin he would willingly lead her to the old woman's cottage.

Being in a desperate plight and not knowing what else to do, the girl agreed. Taking a single precious coin from a small purse, the girl offered it to Toad, who snapped it up ever so quickly and, flicking his tongue like a frog with a fly at hand, stuffed it into his pocket.

Leading the way in his peculiar hopping walk, Toad took the girl on a confusing course along several paths until they came to a very steep drop in the forest floor and the bank of a fast-moving stream too wide and too deep to cross on foot. Parked nearby lay a skiff and pole for ferrying travelers across. Motioning to the skiff, Toad informed the girl that the Cottage was not far on the other side and that he was the ferryman—for another of her coins, he would gladly take her across. When the girl began to protest, Toad told her that he had no choice but to charge her, and that if he didn't, his master would thrash him soundly and not feed him for a week.

The girl was at the mercy of the need and circumstances. Complying, she gave Toad the second of her four coins, which he quickly snapped up like the first.

Then, as skillfully as a frog navigates a lily pad, Toad poled the skiff to the other side of the broad stream. A short distance beyond, he led the girl to the door of a low building that looked more like a long-neglected shack than a cottage. As if expecting a caller, the door swung open and a bent figure appeared, dressed in a long gray dress and so wrapped in a shawl of strange pattern that no hint of the face within could be seen.

"So, my little darling, you have come to bargain with this poor old woman for a potion to cure your sick mother?" the voice asked, sounding kindly enough.

"Why, yes," the girl responded.

"And so you shall get what a little darling like yourself deserves. But you see," the old woman said, raising a finger like a twisted twig, "I'm poor and old and scarcely able to care for myself, so I must charge you a coin for my medicine. But, of course, what is a mere gold coin to the health of your dear, sweet mother?"

Again the girl was at the mercy of need and circumstances. Taking the last two coins from her small leather purse, the girl offered one to the old woman.

Instead of accepting a single coin, the old woman snatched both of them up, saying, "And, of course, another is needed to pay for Toad to ferry you back across the stream."

With that, the old woman disappeared into her hovel and returned with a wide, flat bowl filled with a clear liquid that looked more like rainwater than medicine. "Now you take this, darling, and hurry back to your sweet mother. But mind you, don't spill a single drop, because with each drop lost, you'll reduce its potency."

The old woman carefully handed the bowl to the girl, then disappeared into her shack, banging the door behind her with a vicious laugh. The girl was left no choice but to try to find her way home carrying the potion as best she could without spilling a drop. But, of course, if you've ever tried to carry a wide, flat bowl full to the brim across the kitchen floor, much less along a forest full of tree roots, stones, and sharp grades, you know that it is quite nearly impossible. The young girl managed only a careful step or two before a single drop splashed over the side, which upset her so much that she stopped short and several more drops followed the first.

From there on, things went progressively worse. The trip back across the stream in the rocking skiff and the sharply steep upgrade of the path on the other side took a heavy toll on the contents of the bowl, and on the poor girl as well. The girl became so frantic with each spillage that by the time she had journeyed to where Sprout found her, she had stumbled one last time and the bowl was emptied.

"So you see," the girl with the golden hair said, motioning to the empty bowl at her side, "I have lost all the potion and all my mother's savings as well. I've messed things up so badly, and I'm so worried about my mother that now even if I could find the Good Wizard, I would have nothing to pay him with." The girl hid her face in her hands and began to weep again.

If you haven't guessed by now, the old woman wasn't exactly as kind as she tried to appear. It is an unfortunate fact of life that some people are far less than what they appear to be. For whatever reason, some people grow up all twisted and turned in upon themselves so that they act badly, or are "bad acts," depending on how you arrange your words. Bad-acting people are those who *do* bad things. They are people whose lives are ruled by verbs like *lying, cheating, stealing, tricking,* and many others. Which, I'm sure you and I know, are things *not* to do.

Anyway, this particular old woman, whose face was hidden in the shawl, was actually the Wicked Old Hag of the forest. Wicked hags are the worst kind of bad-acting people because they are very clever at acting badly. They make their living at the expense of others, and that is a very bad act.

The tears of a beautiful young girl in distress is enough to move a mountain to march to the sea, or a knight to venture forth on an impossible mission, and more than enough to cause Sprout to do things he never thought were within him.

Sprout knelt by her side and asked ever so warmly, "What is your name?"

The girl turned her face upward and it shone with the brightness of the sun rising on a summer morn. "I am called 'Dawn,'" she said.

No name was ever more fitting than hers.

"Listen to me, Dawn," Sprout said, with a tone that was well beyond his years. "If you will wait here, I will do what I can to fetch your savings back from that wicked old hag and then together we will find the Wizard. That is an oath, or my name isn't 'Woodsprout.'" And, of course, his name was Woodsprout, and an oath is an oath, and that is the most serious kind of promise anyone can make.

Turning to go, Sprout noticed a large owl that had been sitting on a nearby tree limb all the while. And as Sprout headed down the path, with his green cap and feather and his pack with his red book in it, the owl took off in flight and disappeared among the treetops.

Chapter 6
A Gem of a Predicament

It wasn't long before Sprout came upon a squat fellow sitting upon the edge of the path. This, Sprout thought, must be Toad. Without hesitation Sprout walked up to him and commanded, "Take me to the old woman, and be quick about it. I have business with her."

Toad was so taken back by the brash manner of this young lad that he hopped back a step. Eyeing Sprout suspiciously, Toad wondered if there might not be something more to this boy than a bright green cap with a tall feather.

"Well, let's be on with it," Sprout demanded.

Deciding there was nothing particularly menacing about Sprout, Toad ventured to profit from the situation by asking payment for his services.

"Payment!" Sprout exclaimed. "My business with the old woman is so important that if you delay me any longer and don't take me to her immediately I'll have her turn you into more of a toad than you already are."

To get him to do her bidding, the Old Hag had threatened Toad with doing just that on several occasions. Even though Toad wasn't actually sure the Hag could, he didn't want to find out, and delaying this impatient lad might just make her mad enough to try.

In his hop of a walk, Toad led Sprout down to the stream and the waiting skiff. Once on the other side, Sprout ordered Toad to fetch the Old Hag and bring her out. Soon the Wicked Hag appeared wrapped in her shawl and leaning on a twisted walking stick as bent as she was. Immediately, Toad took his place at the hem of her skirts, cowering there like a mistreated pet.

"A second little darling come to seek the help of a poor old woman, and all on the same day," the Hag said in a voice like crackling leaves. "Isn't that nice, Toad?"

When Toad did not answer her immediately, the Hag gave him a vicious swat with her cane. She was not only a wicked hag—she was a very cruel master.

Never quite used to the Hag's abuse, Toad's eyes flashed anger and hate. But instead of risking another painful swat, and not wanting to incur something, perhaps, far worse, Toad stroked the Hag's skirts and said, "Why, yes, it is nice to have another guest, and I'm sure you'll help if you can."

"It's not help I want," Sprout stated strongly, even though he was not feeling as sure about himself as he had when he first made his oath to Dawn. But for good or ill, he had made his promise. "I'm here to do business."

"Business is it?" the Hag said with a nasty chuckle from beneath her shawl. "And what business could a bold young darling have with a poor old woman?"

As all boys his age, Sprout did not like being referred to as a "darling" and it gave him added courage to do what he had planned.

Reaching into his backpack, Sprout produced a little leather pouch of the kind used as a purse to carry coins or gems or other such objects of value. He held it aloft and shook it enough to make a suitable sound. "You see, I've a bag of stones, stones that will build a palace."

Toad's eyes grew wide and showed greedy expectation. The Old Hag's eyes remained hidden beneath her shawl and showed nothing.

"So the darling has precious gems, does he?" the Hag asked. "And you wish to trade them for something that I have, eh?"

Sprout managed a nod, though the tone of the Hag's voice was quite unsettling.

"And what price does the darling want for his little bag of stones? Stones that could pay the price to build a palace?" the Hag asked, stepping a little closer to Sprout.

"I should think a fair price would be four gold coins," Sprout stated, trying to sound confident and businesslike. Sprout had heard that more than even gold, hags have a particular greed for precious gems and would give almost anything for them.

"A bag of gems for four gold coins; does that sound a fair price to pay, Toad?" the Hag said, patting the squatting figure on the head. "I hope our darling boy is willing to pay fairly for the coins. One should always be fair to a poor old woman, and fair is the price that should be paid." While the Old Hag spoke, she inched closer still.

Sprout pressed on. "By your word, is it a deal? My purse of stones for the four gold coins?"

Sprout had borrowed the small leather pouch from Dawn, and from the path, he had picked up a few ordinary pebbles. Because hags were supposed to love gems more than anything else, Sprout planned to take full advantage of that greed and fool the Hag into believing that the purse was full of gemstones of a precious kind. The Hag had tricked Dawn, and in his desire to help, Sprout saw no reason why he should not, in turn, trick the Hag. But now Sprout was wishing he had thought through his plan a little better before jumping into it so quickly.

"Besides my four gold coins, the darling now wants my word too! How quickly the price goes up," the Hag said. "Let me see the so, so precious stones first."

"It is only fair that I see the coins first," Sprout returned.

The Old Hag let out a chicken cackle of a laugh that did much to further shake Sprout's confidence. Sprout was fast learning that trying to fool a clever old hag with many years of fooling experience is a foolish thing all by itself.

"You want my word, my coins, and now my fairness too? Such a hefty price for a bag of stones!" With her sinister expression concealed, the hag turned her shawl-covered head toward Toad. "My! My! If I suspected that this darling boy was trying to trick a poor old woman like myself, I might guess that what was actually in the bag was more the kind of stone used in building palaces than the kind of stone that would buy a palace."

What the Hag said was true enough. As men reckon value, precious gemstones like diamonds, rubies, and sapphires are worth enough to buy a palace, but, in themselves, are not much good as building material. But good building stone, like granite and the pebbles in Sprout's pouch, isn't considered worth much. The reckoning of value is a funny thing.

"Any darling who would try to trick a poor soul like me should pay a dear price, shouldn't they, Toad?" the Old Hag asked. It took a whack from her cane to get Toad to mumble a yes. Even Toad did not like to think what the Old Hag might do to someone who tried to trick her.

At this point, Sprout realized how foolish his plan was—not his desire to help Dawn but the way in which he went about it. And the only way he could think of to get out of this sticky situation was to turn and run for the skiff in hopes of getting well out into the stream before the Wicked Hag could do whatever it was she intended to do to him. But Sprout wasn't sure he could even walk, much less run. From under her shawl-covered head, the Hag's unseen gaze made his feet feel as if planted in clay flowerpots.

The Hag reached into her skirts, pulled out a small purse of her own filled with Dawn's four gold coins and dangled it from her spidery hand. "If the darling wants to trade for this, I should think that what he's carrying in his little backpack might be a fair and fitting price. What would the darling say to that?"

Sprout's face held the look of a boy caught in his own pickle jar.

"Well, my little darling, will you trade what you have in your pack for this bag of coins and passage back across the stream?"

The decision Sprout then had to make was the most difficult ever. To give up his beautiful red book, the book of his all-too-short life that he had only just begun to fill, for a bag of four coins? All the gold coins in the world would not have been enough. But the coins were for golden-haired Dawn to buy medicine for her sick mother. It was a dear price to ask of a young boy feeling all too foolish.

Finally, Sprout decided that as dear as his life book was to him, Dawn's need was greater still.

Taking his pack in hand, Sprout was about to give it up into the Old Hag's outstretched arms when something totally unexpected happened. The large owl that Sprout had seen earlier suddenly swooped out of a nearby tree, and flying on a straight, sure-winged course, it headed straight at the Old Hag, who was facing the opposite direction. Just when it would have flown smack into the Old Hag, the owl pulled up sharply and with an outstretched talon yanked the shawl from atop the Hag's head and shoulders, then soared upward.

The Old Hag was taken so unawares that for a moment she stood frozen like a molded figure of snow. Without her shawl to hide beneath, the bright shining rays of the sun showed her for what she really was, just a wicked old hag.

Wicked, bad-acting people are always most dangerous and clever when they remain hidden so that others can't see them for what they really are. And likewise, when people are able to see clearly how bad acting and twisted the wicked are, people lose all fear of their wickedness and tend to find them merely quite detestable.

As all wicked people are when caught without their cover, the Old Hag became very frightened. Her ability to scare and control others with deception passed like a fleeting dark cloud. Dropping the bag of coins and her cane, the Old Hag shrieked in a most ear-piercing way and tried to cover her head with her spindly arms. But to no avail. In the full light of day, she was just a wicked old hag with no shawl to hide beneath. Even Toad, whose darkened heart had not been totally bent, realized the Old Hag to be a most loathsome creature for all the bad and wicked acts that she had committed upon undeserving folk like Dawn.

So irate did Toad become for the Old Hag's cruelty to him and the bad things she had gotten him to do that he picked up the Old Hag's cane and raised it to give her what she had so often given him, a good whack. Seeing what was about to befall her, the Old Hag took off in a fearful shriek after the owl and her shawl. With Toad hopping after her, the Hag ran to the base of a large tree in which the owl was perched high above with her shawl.

At first Sprout was shocked to see such wickedness exposed. But when he saw Toad's malice, and the Hag's fearful anguish at being shown for what she was, Sprout felt a sudden surge of pity. As good as it was to feel pity for another, no matter how little the person actually deserves it, Sprout remembered Dawn's need first. Seeing the bag of coins lying on the ground, Sprout snatched it up and ran to the skiff lest the Old Hag regain her precious shawl. But Sprout found he could not quickly undo the clever knot with which Toad had tied the skiff to an iron ring in a log. Remembering his pocketknife, Sprout cut the rope, and with a push of the pole, he set the skiff out into the stream.

In afterthought, Sprout tossed the pouch of pebbles back onto the ground. A fair deal can be getting what you want, as in Sprout's case, or it can be getting what you deserve, as in the Old Hag's case.

With some difficulty, Sprout managed to navigate the craft to the other side. All the while Toad could be seen chasing the Old Hag round and round the tree, the Old Hag shouting up at the owl to give her shawl back.

Finally, Sprout found his way back to Dawn, who sat on the edge of the path waiting as patiently as could be expected for his return. Proudly, Sprout came up to her and handed her the pouch of coins.

Dawn's eyes rose bright and clear upon her face like twin suns above the horizon. So grateful was she to have the coins returned and for Sprout's valiant help that she jumped up and planted a kiss upon his cheek.

Young boys love to receive all kinds of gifts, but a kiss from a pretty young girl is a gift of the most troubling sort. It is a most precious thing, indeed, but it is also an altogether impossible gift to know how to receive. Sprout turned the color of a ripe plum, flushed with the warm juices that make a most head-spinning wine.

"How did you ever manage to get the coins back?" Dawn asked.

"With the help of an owl," Sprout said.

"An owl?"

Sprout told Dawn of all that had happened in as much detail as he could remember. As he was finishing, the very same owl glided out from among the treetops and set down upon a tree stump not far from where they stood.

"There it is!" Sprout shouted.

"Such a large owl too," added Dawn, rising to approach the magnificent creature.

Sprout stopped her by saying, "I don't think we should disturb it. There is something far more to that creature than just being a very large bird."

For a long while, they stood studying the bird from a distance, but the bird appeared to take no notice of them. Finally, Dawn said, remembering her mother's need, "How will we ever find the Wise and Good Wizard, if he lives in this wood at all?"

That was a problem that Sprout had not thought about at all since going to retrieve the coins. It also occurred to Sprout that he himself was lost with no clear idea of how to find himself, much less the Wizard.

Feeling dejected, Sprout sat down to ponder the situation. Dawn sat down beside him, feeling hopeless despite Sprout's valiant return of the coins.

"Oh, we are lost, aren't we, Sprout?" Dawn said with a heavy sob.

"Lost?" a voice boomed, followed by a very gleeful childlike laugh. "Lost is just the other end of found, and if you follow it like a string, you'll always find 'found' at the other end of 'lost.' And besides, you found each other, which is something, and surely that must be counted as a 'find' rather than a 'loss.'"

Jumping to their feet, Sprout and Dawn turned to see that where the owl

52

had been now stood a tall, straight figure clothed in a long robe and hood, blending all the colors of the forest at once, and yet no specific color at any moment.

At first, Sprout and Dawn were a bit frightened. The figure seemed to have appeared out of nowhere. His face, like the Old Hag's, was hidden.

Perhaps sensing their caution, the figure threw back his hood to reveal a face strong and venerable, with eyes sparkling bright like stars in the depth of the night, forever old, forever young. Again he laughed as a child who ever sees the world as a wondrous playground.

Sprout was so amazed and curious that he could not help but ask, "Are you the owl? Or was the owl you?"

Again laughter, then a voice with the depth of all the seas. "Wisdom takes many forms, as you can see, if you bother to look."

"Are you the Good Wizard of the Forest?" Dawn asked hopefully.

"I am both the Wizard and the Forest. One being the other and both the same. Yet, I'm not sure if I am exactly either if your words are the same as their meanings."

Sprout was beginning to feel that the Wizard was like the Old Hag in that both were very clever and not at all easy to understand. But unlike the Old Hag, the Wizard used his words to show truth, not hide it.

"I want to thank you for helping me, if it was your help that I received," Sprout said, respectfully.

"It was, indeed, my help, and your thanks are duly accepted, though good deeds are their own best reward," the Wizard returned, with a short bow.

"I thought I was in dreadful danger from that wicked old hag, and I suppose I had been a little foolish in trying to trick her!" Sprout said.

"Danger, yes," the Wizard said, "but not from her. That Old Hag is harmless enough if you can see her for what she is.

"The danger was in yourself for trying to fool her, because that was just the sort of trick that she would play. Trying to deceive a deceiver is a sure way to become a deceiver yourself. And deceivers soon become wicked. The best way to fight deception is not with more deception but with truth. As the lifting of her shawl."

"Do you mean that I was foolish to try to help Dawn?" Sprout asked.

"Oh my, no! Your reason was good and just. It was your method that was a little foolish. It would have been wiser to choose a course of truth over deception. What you did was like seeing someone who falls into a pond and can't swim. Intending to act well, you jump in to help without remembering that you yourself can't swim. Wisdom comes with knowing what is a good way to act and then acting that way. Helping, telling the truth, giving, loving are all the beginnings of wisdom. Then true wisdom comes with knowing how to do those things well, and in what way, and at what time."

"How should I ever learn that?" Sprout asked.

"By watching how a bird raises her chicks, or how a tadpole learns to swim," the Wizard instructed.

With a flair of his robe like the flapping of powerful wings, the Wizard leaped from the tree stump to the ground and said, "Perhaps more on that later, but for now, Dawn here has a need. Follow me and in due course we shall see what I can do about that."

"But how did you know about Dawn's need?" Sprout asked.

"The same way you know how many fingers you have on your right hand, and what all the toes on your left foot are doing," the Wizard answered.

Chapter 7
Strawberries, Cream and Wizards

Sprout, with his bright green cap and feather and his red book securely in his pack, followed Dawn and the Wizard to a small grassy clearing in the wood. On the edge of the clearing, beneath the overhanging boughs of the trees, stood a small cottage as nice as any. When they entered, Sprout was amazed to find that the inside was very large and spacious with a lofty ceiling. As unbelievable as it sounds, the interior was many times larger than it should be as measured from the outside.

"How—" Sprout began to ask. But before he could, the Wizard answered him.

"As you can see, this cottage holds a lot, a lot more than is really possible. But SHHH!" the Wizard cautioned. "I don't want the outside to know how large the inside is or it will get jealous and want to take up far more area than it already does."

Wise and good wizards are truly marvelous and quite magical in their ways because goodness, coupled with wisdom, can make all sorts of things possible that most would never imagine.

The interior of the cottage was filled with strange gadgets and peculiar paraphernalia that neither Sprout nor Dawn understood in the least. But that is to be expected inside a Wizard's home, and, all in all, it was a very pleasant place to be.

"Before I can do anything of a wizardly sort, I should think a good meal is in order," the Wizard announced.

At that Sprout remembered that he was very hungry and that it was the haste of his hunger that had brought him into the Old Forest in the first place. And despite her worry for her mother, Dawn, too, was of the same mind.

Opening what appeared to be an ordinary cupboard, the Wizard took out a tray laden with hot steaming biscuits and placed it on the table. Reaching into the same cupboard, he then brought forth various earthen crocks containing golden, sweet honey; cool, white milk; ripe red strawberries; and an endless supply of thick, rich cream.

Eating as they did of the most delicious foods ever, neither Sprout nor Dawn could make the slightest dent in the generous board that seemed to multiply in the bowls as quickly as it passed into their smiling mouths.

The food, the air, the smells, the sounds—all held a special magical quality that was evident everywhere but hard to put a name to or a finger on.

When all the corners of their stomachs were neatly and carefully packed like mother's good china in a storage chest, Dawn asked ever so politely if the Wizard could do something for her mother.

With a gentle, concerned smile, the Wizard said, "Do not fret while you are in my cottage. I've sent help to watch over your mother until you return with the medicine that I shall prepare for you."

"Then you'll help? Oh, that is wonderful," Dawn cried aloud. "Thanks to Sprout and the owl, I still have coins to pay you with."

With a laugh, the Wizard threw a strawberry straight up into the air, where it looked to hang a very long time, spinning and sparkling in the light from a nearby window. Then falling suddenly, the strawberry disappeared into the Wizard's waiting mouth.

"If you remember the Forest as a good place," the Wizard said, "and leave a few breadcrumbs when you can at the forest's edge for the creatures to eat, it will be more than payment enough."

Dawn rose, and coming up to the Wizard, gave him a thankful kiss upon the cheek. At once, in the nearby trees outside, birds broke into song, and in the corner of the room, a tall harp began to hum a tune like water falling joyfully along a stony brook.

With a broad smile, the Wizard said, "Such a generous gift for an old wizard makes my ancient bones rattle like chimes in the wind; if I don't sing you both a song to still them, I am afraid that their rattling will keep me awake all night long."

"Yes, yes, a song please," Sprout and Dawn shouted together.

The Wizard went over to his harp while Sprout and Dawn sat themselves upon stools nearby. Even though his hands never touched the strings, the harp made such beautiful sounds that Sprout could see the music in his mind like dancing rainbows in a spring shower.

The Wizard's voice flowed forth in clear, cool tones. "I'll sing you a song of how Woodsprout met golden-haired Dawn and grew so tall that he turned a toad into a man, lifted a rag from the face of an old hag, and let the sunshine into a place in the Forest where a shadow had dwelled."

The verses went on to tell the complete tale of Sprout's adventure, an adventure that Sprout hadn't realized at the time was an adventure. But that is often the way with adventures; you don't really know you've had one until it's over and skillfully woven among the notes of a good song.

The tale, as sung by the Wizard, was so delightful to hear that tears came to everyone's eyes. Even the breeze that blew through the cottage windows was so moved by the song that it carried it out into the Forest for all to enjoy.

The Wizard then sang songs about various forest creatures. The centipede who spent half his life trying to cross all his legs at once, and the other half trying to uncross them. There was another one about the vanity of bald eagles, who always fly near the roof of the sky so that no one can see the top of their heads, even though they aren't really bald at all. And a song about a bear who wanted to be a bird until he found what he thought was an egg to sit upon, but which turned out to be a wasp's nest. The bear quickly decided that it was better to be just what he was, a bear.

There was a story of one forest creature who was so jealous of flowers and the attention flowers received because of their fragrant smells that Nature finally gave the creature a distinctive smell of his own. That was how skunks came to be and why other creatures don't like to be around skunks and their reward for jealousy. And a song about how certain trees, wanting to keep their beautiful leaves year-round, learned to curl them up so tightly that they wouldn't fall off during the harsh winter winds, but then found that, come spring, no matter how hard they tried, the pine trees couldn't uncurl them again.

All the Wizard's songs were fun to hear and taught lessons showing that the creatures in the forest were in many ways like people and that from the forest creatures, people could learn to behave better and become a little wiser.

Even though Dawn and Sprout pleaded for him not to, the Wizard ended his songs.

"So, Sprout, have you heard much in my songs that is worth putting into your book of life?" the Wizard asked.

Sprout had been so caught up in the things that had happened that he hadn't added a single word to his book since the Library. It was a shame not to have written down all the Wizard's marvelous songs, especially the one about Sprout himself, Dawn, and the Old Hag.

The Wizard reassured Sprout that before leaving there would be enough time to record as much as he wanted, and that Sprout and Dawn could come again to his cottage and learn to hear forest songs for themselves. That made Sprout and Dawn very happy, indeed.

"Is there anything that you wanted to add to your book this day that you did not find?" the Wizard asked.

Immediately Sprout recalled the Flagon Slayer.

"I would have liked to have found a real hero to write about," Sprout admitted with just a hint of disappointment.

The Wizard smiled. "Why, Sprout, you did find a hero this day in a place where true heroes are always found, but where few people ever expect to find them."

"I did?"

"Of course!" the Wizard replied.

"And where was that? I don't remember meeting one," Sprout said, feeling a little lost.

"The best heroes don't remember themselves as heroes, and where you found one was in the most unexpected place: within yourself."

Sprout's face hung as if from a clothesline flapping in a breeze.

"Don't you remember, Sprout? You came upon Dawn in need and offered to help. That was a heroic beginning. And had not the owl shown up in the nick of time when things got very tight, you were even willing to give up your life book for the sake of Dawn's need. That was very heroic and noble."

Sprout had not thought that what he had done and what he had been willing to do was particularly heroic. It was just that the circumstances that he had found himself in required him to do those things in order to help Dawn. The feeling of being called heroic made Sprout more than a little uncomfortable.

"It's good that you don't think of yourself as a hero, Sprout, because if you begin to think of yourself as a great hero, you'll run the risk of becoming a flagon slayer."

"How did you know about him?" Sprout asked with new wonder. He had never mentioned the rusty knight to Dawn or the Wizard.

The Wizard chuckled. "When you and Dawn thought you were lost in the Forest, you both referred to me as a wise and good wizard; if I am supposed to be that I'd better know many things that people don't expect me to. You see, wisdom really is quite magical in its own right and can make all kinds of wonderfully magical things happen. Not like wickedness, which can only fool people into believing that it has special power, like the Old Hag."

"But why are there wicked people at all?" Sprout asked, bothered by that particularly troublesome question.

The Wizard's eyes shone with the far-peering clarity of the wisest among the wise, those few who realize the narrowness of mortal wisdom compared to the true depth of God's eternal wisdom.

"That, my dear Sprout, is one of life's unsolvable mysteries. Like why is goodness good? I suspect that goodness is good because that is the way the whole universe is built, out of goodness. If you act in goodness, you act with the universe on your side; you move in the direction in which the universe ultimately flows. On the other hand, I suspect that wickedness is the universe's way of showing us how good goodness is, and it gives us a choice to choose from. Always we are free to choose between goodness and wickedness. When we do show the wisdom to choose goodness over wickedness, it makes goodness all the better. If each of us, by our own choosing, continues to tilt the scales toward goodness, then in the end we'll have a good answer." The Wizard winked at Sprout and then broke out into a long laugh.

While Sprout wrote in his beautiful red book, the Wizard busied himself among his wizardly paraphernalia preparing what would surely be a most wizardly potion to help Dawn's mother. When Sprout was all but finished writing, the Wizard announced that it was best for Sprout and Dawn to get back into things. "Time, you know, is very impatient and doesn't like to wait long for stragglers, or even wizards."

Their stay in the Wizard's cottage had been so much fun, and despite the fact that it had lasted for such a long while, it felt that it hadn't been a stay at all, it had been like a good jolly laugh, too long in coming, too quick in passing. And once outside, when Sprout marked the place of the sun, he discovered it was in exactly the same position as when they had first entered the Wizard's cottage, as if no time had passed. Of course, that is the way of good times, like no time at all, yet always endless.

Sprout then remembered his mother's instructions to be home before dinner. To be late for dinner, even because of an adventure with a wicked hag, a good wizard, and a girl in distress, is no excuse. Mothers are most particular about meals being served and eaten at the proper time. The Wizard understood Sprout's urgency, which just goes to show how truly wise wizards can be.

Once upon the wooded paths, the Wizard, with a wave of his hand, gave Sprout directions that stuck in his mind like taffy on an apple.

"You come back again to the Forest," the Wizard invited. "A Woodsprout is always welcome here, and the Forest is a good place for Woodsprouts to learn and grow, and a better place still to fill pages and pages of a life book."

Sprout thanked the Wizard for the delicious food, the wonderful songs, his help— everything. It's always best to be extra polite to wizards, especially good and wise ones. Lastly, Sprout said goodbye to Dawn, which turned out to be extra hard, even though he wasn't sure why. It would take Sprout quite a few pages more into the future of his book before he would even begin to understand.

As Sprout took off in a trot along the path, the Wizard called after him. "Don't be too hasty or you'll find yourself in the thick of another adventure and you don't have enough time for one before dinner!"

Slowing to a fast walk, Sprout waved back. As the path curved through the forest, the Wizard's fading laugh trailed off into the song of birds in the trees above.

Chapter 8
Happy Endings Make Better Endings

Walking along by himself, Sprout thought about the many experiences and characters he had entered into his book: the Miller, the Knight, the Librarian, the Hag, and, of course, the Wizard and Dawn. And like the many grains of sand that it takes to build a sandcastle, he had gathered a multitude of adjectives, nouns, and verbs;

statements; and even the beginnings of knowledge. But more importantly, Sprout had sampled a taste of the flavor of wisdom, and that was, perhaps, the best of all.

Sprout was sad to close, for now, the pages on his day's journey. But a good book of life is filled with many endings and beginnings. For when an ending is reached, the door is open for a new beginning just ahead. May your life's journey be filled with many endings and beginnings, with good luck and adventure, with words and wisdom, and with a Librarian, a Wizard, and loving parents to guide you.

As he hurried his pace, Sprout could almost smell the aroma of his mother's good cooking, especially the delicious scent of a fresh-baked apple pie cooling on the windowsill. Faster still, Sprout broke into a full run. Surely it is all right to be hasty in your own backyard when dinner is waiting hot on the table.

Like the few pages of this story, all life books will end with a happy, loving home in sight.

For you, and me, and Sprout, it's all in a day spent writing the book of life.

THE END

About the Author

Richard Gleason 1952-2009

Richard was born in Pittsburgh, Pennsylvania, in 1952. His father, Jack, worked as a sales manager for a life insurance firm, which required the family to move several times across the country. In 1964, Richard, age twelve; his parents, Jack and Phyllis Gleason; and sister, Colleen, moved to Gilbertsville, Pennsylvania. Richard's parents had decided to purchase a one-hundred-year-old taproom called Fagleysville Hotel to pursue their lifelong dream. This restaurant would become a fine dining mecca and provided some very formative connections for Richard's future.

From a young age, Richard had a great passion for adventure and learning. These pursuits are evident through his lifelong love of skiing, scuba diving, and backpacking as well as writing, Eastern philosophy, and religion. At an early age, he joined the Boy Scouts and developed an interest in martial arts, specifically Tae Kwon Do. As an accomplished third-degree black belt, Richard competed in the Pan American Games in the 1970s.

His high school years were spent attending The Hill School, a prestigious private prep school located in Pottstown, Pennsylvania. He spent weekends working in the family restaurant and interacting with its many distinguished guests. Richard often brought friends home to stay while their parents were off on exotic holidays. Not wanting them to spend a holiday alone at the school, Richard would instead bring them to hang out at the family's busy restaurant.

After graduating from The Hill School, he went on to continue his education at American University in Washington, DC. This choice was inspired by his mother, who graduated from the university in the 1940s with a degree in chemistry. Richard majored in philosophy and religion to continue his quest for the meaning of life.

Richard left American University after two years to travel to the Far East. This experience became a spiritual quest for him, leading to a deeper understanding of the world. At twenty-one years old, he sought the teachings of Eastern philosophy in India, Nepal, and Sri Lanka.

Richard had developed a desire to write during high school at the Hill. After a few years, he completed several manuscripts. When a restaurant customer introduced him to a famous award-winning author, James Michener, the two became fast friends. Michener became a writing mentor, providing insight and inspiration while critiquing Richard's works. On Richard's Far East travels, he visited with Michener at his home in Sri Lanka. These experiences expanded his understanding of the connection between nature and the world.

After returning to Pennsylvania, Richard worked in the kitchen at the family restaurant. His father, Jack, insisted it was time to do something with his life. A regular customer suggested that he pursue economics and finance and offered to help with the cost of his education if Richard came to E. F. Hutton, a brokerage company, upon graduation. Richard accepted the offer and completed a degree in economics from Albright College in Reading, Pennsylvania.

With an engaging personality, Richard excelled in this profession, becoming a senior vice president of wealth management at the company. During these years he met his wife, Mette, married, and had two children, Alyssa and

Brigitte. He was a dedicated father and would often miss a business meeting to attend one of his daughters' activities. He became an avid supporter of the National Boy Scout Council and presided on the board.

Sprout was first published in 1987 by Winston-Derek Publishers. *Sprout* was well received in the literary community and was used as a teaching tool to encourage philosophical thinking in the classroom.

Sadly, we lost Richard in February 2009. While his light left us much too soon, we are blessed to have had the time to share in his warmth, energy, and love. His legacy lives on in our hearts, as well as his writings, which we hope will kindle the intellectual fire within the minds of his readers. Richard will always be remembered for his exceptional integrity and compassion for others, loyalty to his friends, and love for his family.

When evening was fully come, and the moving throng had gone their ways,
   And all was hushed.
   I heard a voice within the temple saying:
   "All life is twain, the one a frozen stream, the other a burning flame,
   And the burning flame is love."

Thereupon I entered into the temple and bowed myself, kneeling in supplication
   And chanting a prayer in my secret heart:
   "Make me, O Lord, food for the burning flame,
   And make me, O God, fuel for the sacred fire.
   Amen."
   —Kahlil Gibran

South Hanover Mr. Kong's Tai Kwon Do

Richard Gleason Early 20s

Richard competing in Martial Arts Competition.

Backpacking trip in Norway.

Richard Gleason with James Michener at Michener's home Sri Lanka.

Winston Derek Publishers
and
Messrs. David Miller and Mark Lacey
of
The Fagleysville Hotel

cordially invite you to an evening of
food, drink, and friends
in celebration of
the publication of Sprout
a novel by Richard Gleason
illustrated by Liza Fleming

Friday, January ___, 1987
Hors D'oeuvre   6:00 P.M.
Dinner to follow
by advance reservation only
R.S.V.P. by Tuesday, January ___
323-1425
$60.00 per couple plus tax and gratuity
$34.00 per person plus tax and gratuity

Dinner
Appetizer – Coquille St Jacques, Lemon Chicken, Quiche Lorraine
Soup – Cream of Cauliflower   Wild Rice
Salad – Boston Lettuce with Orange, Onions, Almonds
          and Lemon Vinaigrette
Entree – Filet of Beef Wellington
          Duckling a la Fagleysville
          Breast of Chicken with Asparagus Mousse
          Poached Salmon Filet with Lemon Butter
Dessert ~   Lemon Tart   Chocolate Mousse
          Vanilla Ice Cream with Chocolate Sauce
Beverage – Mocha Java, Tea, Brewed Decaf

Book signing invitation held at Faglesville Hotel on January 23, 1987

73

Berks financial adviser Richard Gleason is the author of a children's story called "Sprout."

Photo of Richard for Sprout article - married 2 years

Young reader

'Sprout' reminiscent of French tale

If Antoine de Saint-Exupery were alive today, I think that the Frenchman would enjoy Richard Gleason's children's book, "Sprout." In many ways, Gleason's tale of a boy's experience in the world reminds me of Saint-Exupery's children's classic, "The Little Prince."

Most students of French language and culture have had the opportunity to read Saint-Exupery's story of a pilot whose plane lands in the desert in a strange land inhabited by a young boy in search of the meaning of life.

Both books are simple and complex; they are readable on two levels. Young children can understand and appreciate each story on its simpler level as a narrative, while older children and adults can could follow

Karen L. Miller
Sunday Spectrum Editor

the more complex messages and satires.

Gleason, who resides in Bern Township with his wife, Mette, is a vice president of E.F. Hutton & Co., Wyomissing, by day and a writer by night.

His first book is an impressive

effort in an area of publishing where intelligently written and well-constructed children's stories have become less and less common. To think of a recent publication that is not based on a Saturday morning television program is remarkable in itself.

The story begins with a young boy named Woodsprout, called Sprout for short, who is given a red leather volume by his father. The volume is filled with blank pages. His father instructs him to go out in the world and fill the pages with experiences.

Sprout starts his journey, but finds that others that he meets along the way are not as fresh as he is. They have become hardened to life because of their circumstances. They cannot remember when life was as young and clean and new as what

they see in Sprout's eyes.

Sprout knows that he needs words for his book; he begins with adjectives.

The first acquaintance he meets is the Miller. Sprout tries to honor the Miller by asking for some words for his book as if they are precious grains from the elder's mill. But the Miller is, in fact, stingier with his words than he is with his bounty. He offers the young boy adjectives.

But the poor Miller could only think of negative adjectives until the man stops to think about how he is poisoning the young boy's book and mind.

The Miller takes him to see the Dragon Slayer, a knight in tarnished

See Young reader, Page E-18 ♦

Young reader

♦ Continued from Page E-16

armor. The boy wants to write about a hero in his book and the Dragon Slayer is reputed to be just that noun.

But the Dragon Slayer is a drunk and quite full of himself. By now, the young boy realizes without any adult insight that he has been led to a Flagon Slayer. After all, the Dragon Slayer slays something that is only make-believe anyway. Sprout still has no hero, but he has learned a lot about adjectives and nouns.

Sprout decides to look for knowledge to put in his book. He thinks he can find that in the library. The Librarian is a large bellowing fellow who hires a Doorkeep to keep the knowledge in the library. Pretty soon, Sprout sees that keeping knowledge locked up is the same as barring the people from getting into the library.

This, too, strikes Sprout as being rather odd.

With thousands of books and all that free knowledge, why is there a need for knowledge keepers?

Why isn't the Librarian giving the knowledge away without reservation or hesitation?

Instead, Sprout finds the Librarian more interested in putting books in their proper order than putting books in touch with the proper minds.

The Librarian reminds me of adverbs — loudly, pompously, pretentiously, obsessively.

What the Librarian does offer is a syllogism or tricky reasoning. For some young readers, this may be the first time someone creates this kind of deductive reasoning for them.

He says, "If I say that only dwarfs can grow green beards, and that all dwarfs have beards, you can be sure that behind every green beard you will find a dwarf."

It sounds sort of silly, but it is the beginning of getting children to think.

Sprout's experiences continue as he searches — and later finds — a real hero.

The allegorical style helps to simplify the story. For instance, the name, Sprout, is symbolic of a young, growing thing. The illustrations, created by Liza A. Fleming, an art instructor in the Boyertown School District, aid the imagination.

"Sprout." By Richard Gleason. Illustrated by Liza A. Fleming. Winston-Derek Publishers Inc. Nashville, Tenn. 66 pp. $7.95. Ages 7 to adult. The book is available at B. Dalton Booksellers and Moyer's Book Mart.

Editorial review of original book from local newspaper.

Sculpture of Sprout

https://www.thestoryofsprout.com

GLOSSARY

SPROUT: (verb) to begin to grow; shoot forth; (noun) a seedling

Chapter One: A Most Wonderful Gift

- Burdensome: (adjective) difficult to carry out or fulfill; taxing
- Intricately: (adverb) in a very complicated or detailed manner
- Enchanted: (adjective) 1. placed under a spell; 2. filled with delight
- Bewilderment: (noun) a feeling of being perplexed and confused
- Wonderment: (noun) a state of awed admiration or respect
- Perplexing: (adjective) completely baffling; very puzzling
- Quill: (noun) 1. any of the main wing or tail feathers of a bird; 2. the hollow sharp spines of a porcupine or hedgehog
- Adornment: (noun) a thing which adorns or decorates; an ornament

Chapter Two: A Matter of Adjectives

- **Adjective:** (noun) a word to describe a noun
- **Milled Grain:** (noun) grain ground into flour
- **Sarcastically:** (adverb) in an ironic way; intended to mock or convey contempt
- **Woesome:** (adjective) expressing sorrow
- **Loathsome:** (adjective) causing hatred or disgust; repulsive
- **Mournful:** (adjective) feeling, expressing, or inducing sadness, regret, or grief
- **Belaboring:** (verb) arguing or elaborating in excessive detail

- **Toiling:** (verb) working extremely hard or incessantly
- **Racked:** (verb) caused extreme physical or mental pain to
- **Intolerable:** (adjective) unable to be endured
- **Insufferable:** (adjective) too extreme to bear; intolerable; having or showing unbearable arrogance or conceit
- **Indifferent:** (adjective) having no particular interest or sympathy; unconcerned
- **Avalanche:** (noun) a mass of snow, ice, and rocks falling rapidly down a mountainside
- **Bearing:** (adjective) carrying weight or load
- **Wholesome:** (adjective) conducive to or suggestive of good health and physical well-being
- **Growthsome:** (adjective) conducive to growth; fertile
- **Virtuous:** (adjective) having or showing high moral standards
- **Courteous:** (adjective) polite, respectful, or considerate in manner
- **Gracious:** (adjective) courteous, kind, and pleasant
- **Belligerent:** (adjective) hostile and aggressive
- **Diligent:** (adjective) having or showing care and conscientious in one's work or duties
- **Flagon:** (noun) a large container in which drink is served, typically with a handle and spout

Chapter Three: Flagons and Dragons

- **Inexplicable:** (adjective) unable to be explained or accounted for
- **Bestowed:** (verb) conferred or presented an honor, right, or gift
- **Nuisance:** (noun) a person, thing, or circumstance causing inconvenience or annoyance
- **Midsummer's Eve:** (noun) celebration of the longest day of the year (June 21) in the northern hemisphere
- **Evict:** (verb) expel someone from a property, especially with the support of the law

- **Labyrinth:** (noun) a complicated irregular network of passages or paths in which it is difficult to find one's way; a maze
- **Ale:** (noun) a type of beer or drink
- **Cowering:** (verb) crouch down in fear
- **Irate:** (adjective) feeling great anger
- **Temperament:** (noun) a person's nature
- **Extinguished:** (verb) put an end to; cause a fire to cease to burn

Chapter Four: Knowledge and Dancing Elephants

- **Lanky:** (adjective) ungracefully thin and tall
- **Askew:** (adjective) not in a straight or level position
- **Calamity:** (noun) an event causing great and often sudden damage or distress; a disaster
- **Vaulted:** (adjective) having an arched roof or ceiling
- **Unfathomable:** (adjective) incapable of being fully explored or understood
- **Prestidigitation:** (noun) magic tricks performed as entertainment
- **Prevarication:** (noun) deliberate act of deviating from the truth; intentional vagueness or ambiguity
- **Presbyopia:** (noun) farsightedness caused by loss of elasticity of the lens of the eye, typically happens in middle and old age
- **Primulaceous** (adjective) of or pertaining to the plant group primulaceae or primrose (a type of flower)
- **Valid:** (adjective) having legal efficacy or force
- **Incantation:** (noun) a series of words said as a magic spell or charm

Chapter Five: A Very Long Shortcut

- **Cognizance:** (noun) knowledge, awareness, or notice

Chapter Six: A Gem of a Predicament

- **Predicament:** (noun) a difficult, unpleasant, or embarrassing situation
- **Menacing:** (adjective) suggesting the presence of danger; threatening
- **Bidding:** (noun) the ordering or requesting of someone to do something
- **Malice:** (noun) the intention or desire to do evil; ill will
- **Anguish:** (noun) severe mental or physical pain or suffering
- **Skiff:** (noun) a shallow, flat-bottomed open boat with a sharp bow and square stern
- **Horizon:** (noun) the line at which the earth's surface and sky appear to meet
- **Valiant:** (adjective) possessing or showing courage or determination
- **Gleeful:** (adjective) exuberantly or triumphantly joyful
- **Venerable:** (adjective) accorded a great deal of respect, especially because of age, wisdom, or character
- **Deceive:** (verb) cause someone to believe something that isn't true
- **Tadpole:** (noun) the young fishlike stage of a toad or frog

Chapter Seven: Strawberries, Cream, and Wizards

- **Wizard:** (noun) a man who has magical powers, especially in legends and fairy tales
- **Gadget:** (noun) a small mechanical or electric device or tool, especially an ingenious or novel one
- **Peculiar:** (adjective) strange, odd, unusual; special
- **Paraphernalia:** (noun) miscellaneous articles, especially equipment needed for a particular activity
- **Troublesome:** (adjective) causing difficulty or annoyance
- **Universe:** (noun) all existing matter and space considered as a whole
- **Ultimately:** (adverb) finally; in the end
- **Wickedness:** (noun) the quality of being evil or morally wrong

Chapter Eight: Happy Endings Make Better Endings

- **Multitude:** (noun) a large number of something or gathering of people

STUDY GUIDE FOR SPROUT

CHAPTER 1: A Most Wonderful Gift

1. Discuss the meaning of the phrase "a good home is like good growing soil for children."
2. Why did the parents choose to name the boy "Woodsprout"?
3. What do you think of when you say the boy's name, "Sprout"?
4. What was the "most wonderful gift"?
5. How old do you think Sprout was when he received his gift?
6. What did Sprout's father mean when he said to Sprout, "It's time that you begin filling the pages of your life"?
7. What was meant by the phrase "the rest of the story is going to be mostly up to you"?
8. Why was the gift so wonderful to Sprout at first but then bewildering?
9. In referring to the writing of one's own book, discuss the phrase "each page you write can never be erased."
10. What do *you* do when confronted with a task? What did Sprout do?

CHAPTER 2: A Matter of Adjectives

1. What are adjectives?
2. What time of day did Sprout start his journey?
3. What made his usual, familiar walk to town seem new and different on this day?
4. How does a "voice like gravel kicked from a horse's hoof" sound?
5. Was the Miller happy that morning when he came upon Sprout?

6. Discuss the Miller's view of the world.
7. How did Sprout feel after hearing the Miller's adjectives?
8. What made the Miller change his view of his life?
9. Discuss the meaning of "a story begun with good adjectives will have a better ending."

CHAPTER 3: Flagons and Dragons

1. Discuss the statement the Miller made—"what a story that is!"—when he referred to the knight's tale as they entered the tavern.
2. How was Sprout feeling as he entered the tavern? (
3. Act out the knight sitting at his table. (snoring, awakening, drinking, hard to move around, clamoring)
4. Why did one arm of the knight move easily while he could hardly move the other?
5. Discuss the author's meaning of "a knight is a knight, and that should account for something." (What is in a name? Should we live up to a name?)
6. Was the knight's behavior a good example of his rank? (Was he self-involved?)
7. How did the dragon handle things that bothered him? (destructive, made others share the misery)
8. The dragon did not like to be scolded for bad behavior. Discuss your thoughts on this from your personal experience.
9. Did the children make the best of the dragon's bad behavior and destructiveness? How?
10. Discuss the dragon's behavior when the author describes that he "could not stand to have others happy when he was not."
11. What did the author mean by the statement about the knight falling asleep "that comes from a tale too long and too often told"?
12. What was the difference Sprout noticed between the knight he saw and the knight in the tale?

13. Discuss "the difference between a good story and a *good* story." What did the author mean here?
14. What happened that changed the dragon from fierce to afraid? (Bully?)
15. What lesson did Sprout learn from his experience with the knight and his tale? (Be honest.)
16. Why was Sprout disappointed after his experience with the knight?

CHAPTER 4: Knowledge and Dancing Elephants

1. What was Sprout seeking next to add to his book? (truth and knowledge)
2. Where did he go to look for it?
3. Talk about what knowledge means to you.
4. Describe how the library may have looked. (or sketch?)
5. Sketch how the Door-Keep may have looked.
6. What did the Door-Keep and Sprout discover that they had in common?
7. When Sprout came upon the Librarian, what was she trying to do?
8. Why did the Door-Keep wink?
9. What did the author mean when the Librarian said, "The sooner one gets started, the closer one gets to never having it."
10. When Sprout started to understood about the search for knowledge, what did he compare it to?
11. Where did the Librarian say knowledge begins?
12. Give an example of a "true statement."
13. The Librarian taught Sprout an important habit. You _____ before you _____.
14. What are the building blocks of knowledge according to the Librarian?
15. Describe some of the attributes Sprout learned about knowledge.
16. "The true answer to living is a _____."
17. Is gaining knowledge easy or hard?
18. "Being quite _____ is always _____."
19. What is meant by the Door-Keep's statement, "Knowledge needs lots of sunshine to keep it clear and healthy." (It must be applied.)

CHAPTER 5: A Very Long Shortcut

1. Compare how Sprout felt when he left the library to when he left the tavern.
2. Why did Sprout take a shortcut?
3. What important lesson did Sprout learn about haste?
4. When you come to a Y in the "road," how do you think about it?
5. Explain the idea of making a choice between two unknowns or going back along the familiar.
6. Who did the girl say would be the only type of person who could help her?
7. Relate an experience you had, like the girl, where you suddenly felt lost.
8. Why do you think the girl had been so trusting of Toad to honestly help her?
9. What knowledge did the girl gain from her experience with Toad and the old woman? (People may not be what they seem.)
10. How did the old woman make her living? (at the expenses of others?)
11. What did Sprout gain from Dawn's story of Toad and the old woman taking advantage of her? (courage)

CHAPTER 6: A Gem of a Predicament

1. How did Sprout present himself to Toad? (assertive)
2. How did that change how Toad responded to Sprout, and why was that different from Dawn's experience?
3. Explain how something has value and why to one person it is very valuable and to another worth nothing.
4. How would you describe Sprout's decision to give up his red book? (unselfish, heroic, caring?) Was it easy or hard? Why?
5. When the owl swooped down and stole the Old Hag's shawl, what happened to the Old Hag?(took away her confidence and showed all who she really was)

6. How would you describe Sprout's efforts to help Dawn?
7. What did the wizard mean by "lost is just the other end of found"?
8. "Wisdom takes many forms." Explain.
9. How did the Wizard differ from the Old Hag when he spoke?
10. What is meant by "good deeds are their own best reward"?
11. How does the wizard describe wisdom?

CHAPTER 7: Strawberries, Cream, and Wizards

1. Describe the wizard's cottage.
2. What happens when you put goodness and wisdom together? Give an example in your own experience.
3. How did Sprout see the forest at first? What did he learn and how did he feel about it after his experiences with the Wizard?
4. Does a good deed always need monetary payment?
5. What did the wizard call Dawn's kiss on his cheek? (a generous gift)
6. Describe the song the wizard sang.
7. Sprout was hoping for adventure. Did he find it? When did he realize it? (Wizard's song)
8. What else did the song sung by the Wizard teach?
9. What had Sprout thought he had not found that day to write about in his book? (hero)
10. What did the Wizard tell Sprout about finding a hero?
11. What happens when one starts to think of oneself as a hero? (risk of becoming the Flagon Slayer)
12. "Always we are free to choose between _____ and _____." (good and evil, honesty and cheating, happiness and dissatisfaction)
13. How much time did Sprout and Dawn spend with the Wizard? What did it seem like?
14. Why did the Wizard advise Sprout not to be too hasty in his departure?

CHAPTER 8: Happy Endings Make Better Endings

1. List some of the lessons Sprout learned and added into his red book.
2. What did the author mean when he wrote, "all life books will end with a happy, loving home in sight"?

Made in the USA
Middletown, DE
14 July 2023

35009600R00055